Red Thunder

Red Thunder

by
John P. Hunter

Colonial Williamsburg
The Colonial Williamsburg Foundation
Williamsburg, Virginia

18 17 16 15 14 4 5 6 7 8

Cover art by Barbara Leonard Gibson

Map by Elizabeth Eaton

Designed by Helen M. Olds

Library of Congress Cataloging-in-Publication Data

Hunter, John P., 1947–
Red thunder / by John P. Hunter.
p. cm.
Audience: In Virginia in 1781, fourteen-year-old Nate Chandler and his dog Rex join James Armistead Lafayette, a slave, as spies for the Continental Army as the battle of Yorktown and the end of the Revolutionary War approach.
ISBN-13: 978-0-87935-231-8 (alk. paper)
ISBN-10: 0-87935-231-0 (alk. paper)
1. Yorktown (Va.)—History—Siege, 1781—Juvenile fiction. 2. United States—History—Revolution, 1775–1783—Juvenile fiction. [1. Yorktown (Va.)—History—Siege, 1781—Fiction. 2. Spies—Fiction. 3. Slaves—Fiction. 4. Dogs—Fiction. 5. War—Fiction. 6. Virginia—History—Revolution, 1775–1783—Fiction. 7. United States—History—Revolution, 1775–1783—Fiction.] I. Title. II. Title: Secrets, spies, and scoundrels at Yorktown.

PZ7.H91713Red 2007
[Fic]—dc22

2006030730

The Colonial Williamsburg Foundation
PO Box 1776
Williamsburg, VA 23187-1776
www.history.org

Printed in the United States of America

Manufactured by Berryville Graphics, Inc., Berryville, VA
PO #365838 10/17/13
Cohort: Batch 1

For
Will, Matt, and Lilla

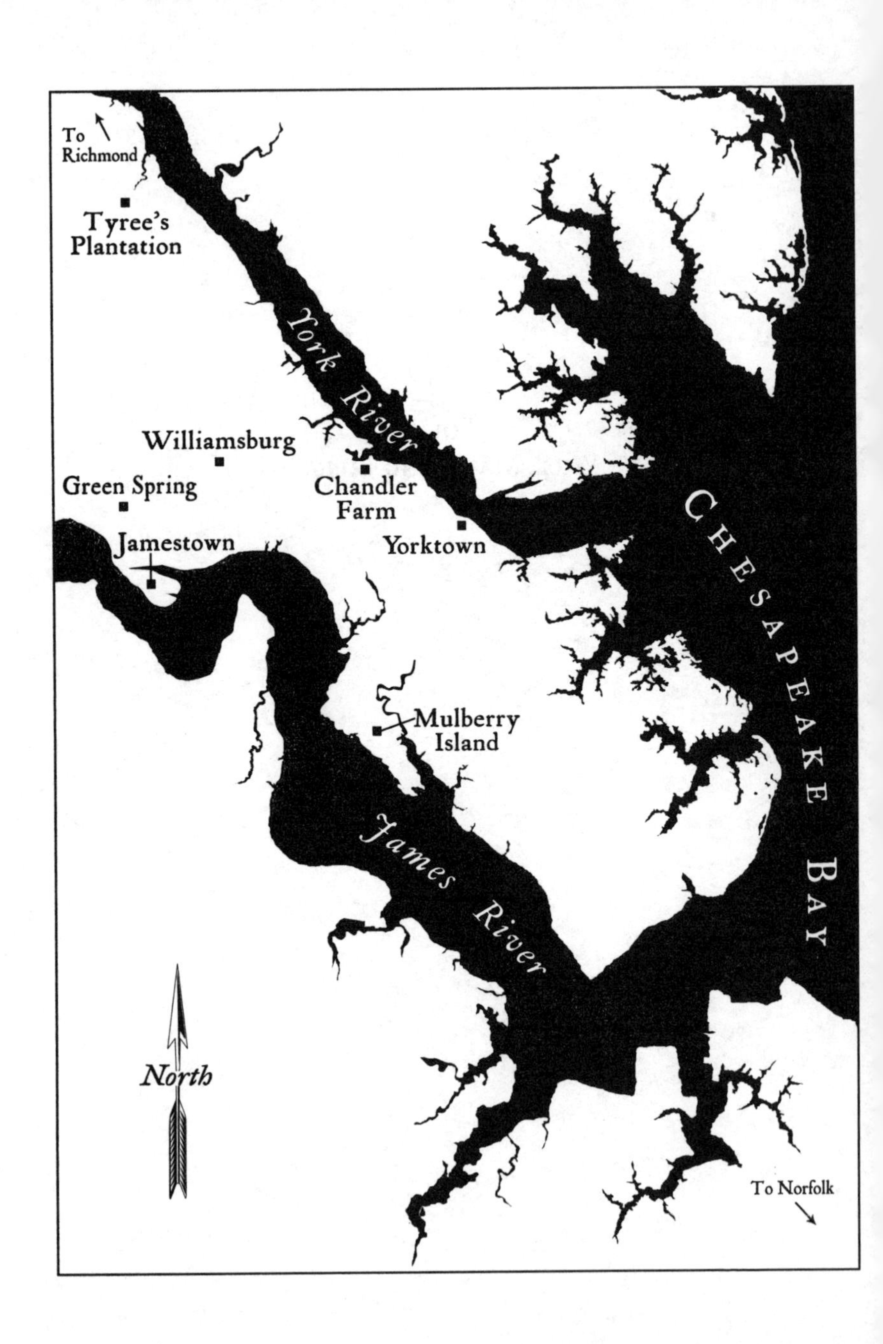

To Richmond
Tyree's Plantation
York River
Williamsburg
Green Spring
Chandler Farm
Yorktown
Jamestown
CHESAPEAKE BAY
Mulberry Island
James River
North
To Norfolk

CHAPTER 1

British dragoon Colonel Banastre Tarleton was only in his twenties, but the war-hardened veterans under his command were terrified of him. There was something in the boyish officer's eyes that could freeze a man. Tarleton led his dragoons on shock missions throughout the Virginia countryside that were distinguished by their ferocity. He took his raids to an unprecedented level of savagery because he enjoyed it.

The lumber mill was in flames as Tarleton led his galloping riders away. Several bodies lay scattered by the building and on the adjacent dam. The only signs of life were the rats running from the fire.

Carrying a herding stick, Nate Chandler rode his horse behind a herd of twenty cows, his big dog, Rex, obediently at his side. Although Nate was only fourteen and looked a year or two younger, he could do the day's work of a man. He had not yet filled out his lanky, awkward frame, and, although he was strong, his muscles were more like lean ropes than the thick oak-root arms of his father. The boy wore a faded old felt hat with a wide brim that covered most of his longish brown hair and shielded his face from the summer sun. His homespun linen shirt and pants had been made by his mother as had every piece of clothing he had ever owned.

On a recent trip into Williamsburg, a heavyset local boy of sixteen had told Nate he looked like a crane walking down the street. Unsure what to make of the comment, Nate went down to the marsh near their cabin after he returned home and observed a crane searching for food among the reeds. After watching the stick-legged creature move around with jerky, unsure movements, he decided the boy had not given him a compliment. Unlike the sharp-featured bird, however, Nate had an open, friendly face highlighted by a gift from his mother: he had inherited her perfectly straight white teeth. Despite his lankiness, it was hard not to be charmed by a simple smile from Nate. His good nature and general contentment with life shone through.

Two of the cows veered off the trail toward some fresh clover. Rex looked up at Nate, ready.

"Cows, Rex," Nate said.

Rex had been only a puppy, a few weeks old, when Nate found him alone, scared, and starving in the woods. There were fur and blood signs that his mother had met a violent end, but Nate had never found her body. The boy's parents were skeptical of providing for a nonworking animal at first, but, soon, his puppy antics and trainability won them over.

"Look at those big paws and powerful chest," William had said. "He'll be a big one. Perhaps too big to be of much use as a herder."

"We'll see about that," Rachel countered. "He's certainly intelligent and seems to have good instincts. He just might turn out to be a fine worker."

"Once he grows," added Nate.

Rex grew. And grew. By the time he was two, the

dog was almost two and a half feet tall at the shoulders standing on all fours. His shoulders and neck filled out, thick and powerful. His legs were long and strong. The light straw color of his puppyhood gave way to a darker gold coat as he aged. Rex's hundred-plus pounds were intimidating but were trumped by his happy-looking face and, surprisingly, sky blue eyes.

William commented that, "Although I had my doubts, and one cannot tell by looking at the animal, there must have been a herder in the family tree and recent. Why, this dog takes to the task like a hog to the wallow."

In response to Nate's command, Rex broke into a trot and moved back and forth between the cows and the clover. With each pass, he moved closer and closer to the cows, darting, angling them away from the clover. The dog was relentless, and the cows finally gave up and moved back into the herd. Rex made a turn around the entire group, tightening it up.

Nate held up his herding stick and pointed it to the right. Rex understood the signal and shepherded the cows through an open gate and into a pasture.

"Good work," Nate said.

He dismounted and lifted the gate logs on the split-rail fence into place. A shrill whistle from over the rise caused Rex's ears to go up and prompted Nate to swing back up on his horse. Nate spurred his mount to a gallop and chased the dog up a gentle green hill.

At the top of the rise, Nate and his horse caught up with the speeding dog and they slid to a stop. Rex rose up on his hind legs and put his feet against the horse's side. Nate rubbed the big gold head and floppy ears while he looked toward the small farmhouse, barn, and outbuildings spread out at the base of the hill.

It was 1781, six long years after the American war for independence from Great Britain had begun. So far, the conflict had not directly touched the farm, but reports of vigorous redcoat activity in Virginia had area residents on edge. Patriots like the Chandlers were not quite sure what to expect if the British army kept moving their way.

The Chandler farm was no fancy plantation, but William Chandler, his wife, Rachel, and their son, Nate, took tremendous pride in their one hundred Virginia acres. They came to the colony from England when Nate was still an infant. The family had a small inheritance from Rachel's father and decided to strike out on their own and make an independent life.

When they arrived in Virginia, William soon realized that the amount of money they had would not buy an operational farm with cleared land, fences, and outbuildings. Farming had been under way in the region for over a hundred years, and the rough wilderness William and Rachel expected turned out to be a settled landscape with the attendant price tag.

An ad they found in the *Virginia Gazette,* placed by an elderly, retired cabinetmaker, set their dream in motion. The old bachelor had purchased a hundred acres forty years prior with a vague notion to one day farm the land, but tending to his thriving business and dabbling in politics prevented him from ever getting around to it. Near the end of his days, the old man was ready to sell the acreage, but not many people were interested in such a small parcel. Especially one that needed to be cleared, had no fences, and backed up to an expanse of marshland. Too much work for most, but not for William and Rachel, and a deal was quickly struck.

Like most rural farmers, Rachel and William had assumed they would have many children to help share the work burden. Shortly after arriving in Virginia, however, Rachel contracted a nearly fatal illness that made giving birth again impossible.

"If the good Lord is to allow us only a single child," Rachel had said, "he certainly blessed us with a fine one."

Their land was eight miles from Williamsburg, toward Yorktown, only a half mile from the York River. The hundred acres was a wild, overgrown tract surrounded by a vast vista of developed farms. After passing by several such operations and then seeing their overgrown, tangled land for the first time, Rachel said with respect, "Those who came before were a tough, strong lot."

"Indeed," William agreed and then boasted, "yet not a whit tougher nor stronger than the Chandlers."

Rachel smiled, nodded, and squeezed her husband's arm with the exciting possibilities of it all.

Before Nate was old enough to help his father, William had hacked out their farm by hand and ax. He had been an average-sized man with a sturdy frame when he started, but, after years of chopping down trees, clearing fields, building fences, and planting crops, he was as thick and powerful as a bull. There were about twenty acres that he left uncleared. They were on a low ridge that sloped down toward the marsh and the creek. It would have been hard land to farm, and, besides, William and his son loved to walk and hunt in the raw beauty of those woods.

Nate had inherited his father's light blue eyes and strong chin but not his stocky build and dark hair. The father wore the same homespun clothing as his son, but he was harder on it.

"How you can wear out a pair of breeches in two months' time is beyond me," Rachel often joked. "Why, keeping a growing boy dressed proper is easier than keeping you decently clothed."

The Chandler fences were always mended, tools were cleaned and put away after use, the livestock was well tended, the garden laid out in straight rows, and firewood stacked as perfectly as palace wall bricks. The small two-room house itself was as clean and neat as a farm cabin could be.

Tarleton and his men pulled up their horses as Sergeant Clinton Adickes and three other men rode up from the opposite direction. While Colonel Tarleton was from an aristocratic family and could move chameleon-like through a royal drawing room, Sergeant Adickes brought his own kind of evil to the field. Despite his dragoon uniform, he looked like what he was—a dirty little thug. His slitlike eyes were cold and cruel. Tarleton was as wicked; he just did not look it.

"Fine herd of cattle three miles hence, sir," Adickes reported to Tarleton, who was impatiently slapping the flat of his sword against his boot. "Wee little house there is, not truly much to bother with save the beef which might well set a fine table."

Anxious for any kind of action, Tarleton shouted, "Yes!" as he bolted away on his huge black horse. The sergeant wheeled his horse around, and he and the rest of the dragoons whipped their mounts after the colonel, who was fast disappearing down the trail.

Another of the shrill whistles seemed to come from inside the barn. With Rex loping ahead, Nate cantered the horse down the hill. Inside the barn, Rachel and William were trying to calm a ewe that was kicking and trying to twist away from them.

Like her son's, Rachel's strength was deceptive. She had the same thin, angular frame as Nate, but she carried it with a fluid grace. Very few women in colonial Virginia went anywhere without a hat or bonnet, but Rachel disliked both intensely. As a result, her Nate-colored brown hair was streaked by the sun in summer and showcased her sparkling brown eyes. She had the posture of a refined lady, but Rachel could chop wood, carry pails of water forever, flip a rowdy calf over on its back, and clean, cook, and sew in between.

"I wish I were a bigger man," Nate had once said to his father as they struggled to roll a big rock from the pasture.

"It will come with time, but size is not here," William replied as he squeezed his son's arm. "It's in there." And he touched a spot over Nate's heart. "For proof, look no further than your mother."

"What's wrong?" Nate asked as he entered the barn.

"The lamb is twisted inside," William frowned. "If Cassie doesn't relax, the movement might well do the both of them in."

"Turn her into my lap," Rachel said to Nate.

As William tried to control the sheep's flailing legs, Nate reached up under the big ewe, got a grip, and shifted her over to Rachel, who was sitting cross-legged on the barn floor.

"That's a sweet old girl," she cooed. "Just calm yourself and you'll soon have a nice new baby."

Being in Rachel's lap seemed to relax the animal. She stroked the wooly head and continued to talk to the ewe in a soft, soothing voice.

"You can try now," Rachel said to William and Nate. "She knows she's in good hands."

While Nate kept a grip on the animal's rear legs, William reached inside and managed to turn the lamb.

"All is well now, Cassie," William said to the ewe. "You can bring her into the world now."

Within only a few minutes, a brand-new lamb was peacefully nursing.

"A pretty one," Rachel praised Cassie. "You did a fine piece of work as usual." And to Nate and William, she added, "I must say, the Chandler men made no small contribution as well."

William took a deep bow. "We are here but to serve, madam."

"Our supreme pleasure to assist in some small way," Nate said as he swooped off his farm hat in a gallant way.

"Well, then, perhaps you both deserve a piece of the hot gingerbread that is this very minute cooling in the. . . . Where is Rex?!"

Colonel Tarleton loved the ritual of a precision cavalry formation prior to a freewheeling charge. Even though they were on a back trail with no audience or need for ceremony, he used his sword as scepter and silently formed his mounted troops into a straight line. A right angle swipe of the blade and the men turned all of their horses as one toward the edge of the woods fronting the road. The young colonel held the sword up high and then lowered it slowly. The Thoroughbred horses started moving like phantoms through the trees.

Rex was not in the barn and neither was Rachel for long. She jumped up and ran from the barn toward the house. William and Nate were close behind.

Inside the main room of the cabin, Rex was busy licking the last remains of hot gingerbread from his muzzle and paws. A completely empty metal pan sat on the floor beside him.

Rachel, Nate, and William rushed in.

"You ate it all?! An entire gingerbread cake?!" a disbelieving Rachel said to Rex.

In a performance worthy of the London stage, Rex turned his blue eyes on Rachel and looked hurt and unimpeachably innocent.

Rachel picked up the pan and banged her hand on it like a drum.

"All of you men, human and dog, get out of my kitchen and go to your work!"

Nate, William, and Rex bolted through the door and back to the fields. Rachel shook her head and tried to suppress a smile.

None of them could have known that, at that moment, something terrible was coming through the woods that would turn their world upside down.

Chapter 2

Nate's next chore was to continue the long process of clearing a new pasture of rocks and stumps with a team of oxen. The boy looked small next to the huge beasts as he urged them to pull a big stump from the ground using a harness and chain.

"Go, Tug, give it all you have! Pull, Big Dan! Pull! Pull!" Nate shouted to the massive animals.

One last powerful lunge and the stubborn stump popped from the ground like a cork from a bottle.

"Good boys!" Nate exclaimed. "Good boys!"

As Nate was unhooking the chain from the stump, something in the tree line at the far end of the field caught his attention. The boy shielded his eyes and squinted. Although he could not make out what it was, the woods seemed to be alive with movement and quick flashes of sunlight reflecting off of something shiny. A warning bell went off in Nate's head, and he felt his stomach muscles clench a little.

Until that day, the most excitement Nate had ever experienced, save the occasional wild pig in the woods, was the bustle of a Williamsburg street. Even that was slow-paced and somehow polite. There was nothing slow-paced or polite about a hundred dragoons resplendently uniformed in special green tunics, instead of the traditional British red, on their giant horses, drawn swords flashing in the morning sun, bursting from the tree line and straight toward him.

Nate did not so much freeze in fear as he turned to stone in awe. Probably a good thing as a dozen whooping riders stormed by him on either side. One of the riders kicked Nate in the chest as he thundered by. Nate collapsed to the ground just as the evil-eyed Sergeant Adickes, no more than four years older than Nate himself, pulled up his horse. For sport, the soldier leaned down and slew the two huge oxen with his sword.

That brutality snapped Nate back up on his feet.

"Tug! Big Dan!"

He stared at the dying oxen and then shot a fierce look up at the smirking soldier.

"Butcher!" he screamed.

Blindly and with no plan at all, Nate charged. Sergeant Adickes laughed out loud and smashed the flat side of his sword against Nate's forehead. Nate's eyes went funny, and he fell over onto the dying oxen.

"Now there be three worthless beasts lyin' in a pile," the sergeant hissed.

He held up his bloody sword and spurred his horse down the field toward the house and the madness.

The crazed dragoons were like a black and green tsunami rampaging over the farm. They were everywhere at once, burning, smashing, killing, destroying any and everything in their path.

Rex had been in a pasture standing guard over his cattle when he heard the ruckus. He took off at full speed, cleared a four-foot-high fence, and bolted across the pasture toward his master. Dizzy from the blow to his head, the boy first staggered, then trotted, then broke into a run down the sloping field and toward the house. Rex ran ahead, barking frantically. Already, the barn and other outbuildings were ablaze.

William ran from the barn, madly weaving through the churning mass of horses and toward the small house and his wife.

"Rachel! Rachel!" William tried to shout over the mayhem. "I'm coming! I'm coming!"

Rachel held a long kitchen knife and stood screaming in the doorway. William did not make it. He dropped to the ground amid a barrage of pounding hooves and slashing weapons. Rachel dropped the knife, and her fists went to her throat. She was in a state of terrified shock, and no more screams would come. She stood like a statue as the cavalrymen trampled through her garden and over her chickens. Four riders pitched flaming tar torches through her treasured glass windows. Then she saw Nate and Rex running toward the house, and something like a scream but far worse pierced through the bedlam. Her son was spattered with ox blood.

Somehow, Nate and Rex maneuvered around, through, and under the horses and made it to the corner of the house.

"Mother!" Nate screamed as he ran to her.

At that moment, Nate saw Sergeant Adickes, holding a flaming torch, spur his horse up the steps. The big horse slammed Rachel to the ground and then plowed into the house.

"No!" Nate yelled through the smoke that was now boiling out through the windows and up from the lower foundation. He took three steps toward his mother but then had to throw himself to the ground to avoid a saber thrust from a dragoon who galloped by. Crawling the last few feet with Rex by his side and barking loudly, he made it to her. His face right next to his mother's ear, Nate spoke in the manic, rushed voice that comes with desperation.

"I will get you away from here," he gasped. "I will get you safe."

Still on his knees, he gathered Rachel in his arms. The wide-eyed boy stood with her and stumbled a few feet out in front of the burning house. Coughing and dizzy from the smoke, Nate sank to the ground with his mother.

"They will go soon, and then we will be well and happy and all will be good," he said in a desperate rapid-fire voice and then had a coughing fit. He felt a weak squeeze on his arm.

Over her cradled head, Nate could see the smoky form of Adickes and his horse smashing and burning everything in the home his mother had kept so well. Nate laid Rachel down gently, and then, in a rage, he jumped up, grabbed the kitchen knife from the ground near the steps, and charged into the house.

Adickes was swinging the fire torch around the walls as the boy took two long steps across the room and slashed the knife into the sergeant's thigh. He let out a scream of pain and dropped both his sword and the torch. Enraged, he wheeled his horse against Nate slamming him against a flaming wall. Adickes drew his pistol and was a millisecond away from shooting Nate in the head when Rex, in one move, jumped to a table and then up onto the sergeant. The pistol went flying, but Adickes miraculously stayed mounted. Rex crashed down to the floor and was kicked several times by the horse, which was severely panicked by the small space and raging flames. The house was becoming an inferno. Dazed, Rex lay motionless in a corner.

Adickes's cocky, evil eyes momentarily went wide and afraid as he looked straight down the barrel of his own pistol. Backlit by a wall of flame, Nate was on his knees holding the pistol with both hands. It was pointed directly at the dragoon's heart.

Nate's hands were shaking badly from fury and the intensity of the past few minutes, but his addled mind remembered something his father had said about pistols. A traveler had tried to sell his father a pistol, but William would not have it.

"Past eight feet, I might as well throw a stone," he had said. "'Tis not the man in Virginia foolish enough to wager a pence on a pistol's accuracy past that."

The boy focused his entire body and mind into holding the gun steady and level. Nate pulled the trigger as he took a deep breath. He inhaled mostly smoke, and that and the boy's head injury saved Adickes's life. As he fired, Nate slumped over forward and crumpled down to the floor. The shot went far wide of its mark. The dragoon laughed, turned his horse, and jumped the terrified animal through the flaming doorway.

Rex was injured but conscious. He dragged across the room to Nate and licked at his face. There was no reaction. Rex managed to stand and gather the neck of Nate's shirt in his mouth. The dog pulled his master inch by inch across the floor and through the dense smoke. A few feet from safety, Nate had a brief moment of consciousness and dragged and pulled along with Rex until they both got out of the burning house and onto safe ground. The last of the cavalrymen disappeared into the woods. Nate immediately passed out. Trembling, Rex sat by him and watched the house turn into a giant fireball and collapse in on itself.

Nate woke up some hours later, but he did not open his eyes. The horror of what had happened was in his head, but some safety mechanism in his brain would not allow him to believe it. He remembered bits of someone lifting him, a hazy ride in a wagon, a soothing voice, but none of that was clear. Maybe it was just a bad dream. The pounding in his head and the smell of the smoke on his clothes told him otherwise. He was on a bed and could feel Rex next to him. Nate put his hand on his dog and sat up. Rex licked his face. It was only then that the boy opened his eyes.

The first thing he saw was his mother with her eyes shut tight with grimace sitting ramrod straight in a chair across an unfamiliar room. A purplish black bruise covered the entire left side of her face and snaked down her neck. Her chest and left arm were securely bandaged and it sounded like every breath she took was torture. But she was breathing!

"Mother!" Nate tried to shout, but it came out as a hoarse whisper.

He stood, but he was so dizzy he had to grab the wall to keep from collapsing to the floor. After a few moments and several deep breaths, he took a few steps across the room and, again, said, "Mother."

Rachel's eyes opened, and the faintest whisper of a smile showed in the corners of her mouth. She mouthed the word "son" but could not speak.

Nate reached out and touched her, but she winced in pain. The boy immediately removed his hand. He could also see why she was sitting straight up in a chair. It was the only way she could breathe.

"I . . . I . . . thank the good Lord you're alive," was all he could think to say.

Rachel nodded, and her eyes said she loved him.

"You will be well and soon," Nate continued.

Rachel nodded.

Although he dreaded the answer, Nate asked, "And Father?"

Rachel cut her eyes toward the door of the small bedroom.

"He's here?! Alive?!"

Rachel's eyes sparkled for a brief second, and the boy knew his father had lived through the ordeal.

How Nate and his parents got to this house was something the boy would never be able to remember clearly, but they all owed their lives to Continental soldiers. A small foraging detachment had been drawn to the farm by the tower of smoke rising up above the trees. When they arrived, the dragoons were gone and the fires were raging. They lifted Nate, William, and Rachel to the back of their wagon and left them at a church in the village of Mulberry Island.

The pastor of the church was a compassionate man who understood his flock. In no time, he had the injured family moved down the street to the home of a spinster, Miss Louisa Albright. Miss Albright had spent most of her life caring for her now-deceased mother and, since, a variety of orphans, sick, elderly, and wounded. It was simply her nature, and she was never happier than when she had someone to take care of. She had expertly dressed Nate's cuts and burns while Dr. Averett, the local physician, had tended to Rachel.

Miss Albright and Dr. Averett were now working on an unconscious William as Nate entered the main room of the house. Miss Albright mopped the sweat from William's face and neck as the stocky man lay motionless on her dining table. Dr. Averett's back was to Nate, but he seemed to be wrapping something.

"How is my father?" Nate whispered as he stepped up to the table.

"You're up and about!" Miss Albright exclaimed in a sweet voice. Her face had an angelic quality. "Now, that is a fine sign indeed."

"My father?"

"He's a tough bird if ever I saw such," Dr. Averett said. "Broken up mightily, but, barring a fever, he should live quite a while past today. His sword wounds will heal, and I hope I can save the leg."

"Save it?"

"Ah, 'tis so. It's as badly broken a limb as I've seen, and I fought the Indians as a young man. I slipped the bone back under the skin. I hope I can save it."

Nate looked down at his father, who was weaker and more helpless than his son could have ever imagined. It was unthinkable that this strong man might lose a leg. He was, however, alive.

"We shall give this bracing and binding a few days and see how it does," Dr. Averett continued.

By nightfall, William had been moved into the room with Rachel. Nate and Dr. Averett picked up Rachel in her chair and moved her to her husband's bedside. Nate slept on the floor but woke up often and listened to the labored yet reassuring sounds of his parents' breathing.

Very early in the morning, when it was still dark, William stirred and cried out. Nate leapt up, and Rachel placed her hand on her husband. William looked up at his wife and son in the moonlight, and the panic in his face and eyes evaporated. He motioned Nate closer.

Although it required monumental effort, William managed to croak out to Nate, "Go . . . to . . . the . . . farm. Save . . . what . . . you . . . can."

"I'll not leave you nor mother, sir," Nate responded in as strong a voice as he could muster.

"Yes . . . you . . . will. It . . . is . . . all . . . we . . . have," William gasped and then passed back out.

Rachel looked at Nate, and her eyes said, "Go."

At sunrise, Nate was waiting for Dr. Averett when he came by to check on his patients. The doctor assured the boy there was nothing he could do to help his parents or even make them more comfortable.

"My feeble efforts have been expended. Now, time is the only real remedy," Dr. Averett said. "And it will take a great deal of that. In the days to follow, your mother and father will be in the best of hands. Miss Albright has the touch. The good Lord put something in her hands that brings people back."

"We have no money," Nate said.

"Nor would she take it if you did. Miss Albright was put on this earth to nurture, and, to my old eyes, she has no peer and does it joyfully."

Nate felt better about leaving. He kissed his mother's unbruised right cheek, touched his sleeping father's hand, and left by midmorning. It was late afternoon when Nate limped up to the still smoldering pile of black sticks that had been his family home.

With Rex close by his side, Nate walked the farm looking for anything worth saving. He walked to the furthest outbuilding, the smokehouse. It was a pile of smoldering rubble. The ten fine Virginia hams that had been hanging from the rafters were nothing more than crunchy little balls of coal. Rex found a side of bacon in the debris, but it too was severely burned. Rex sniffed at the meat and took a bite. The bacon fell apart in a shower of black flakes.

Even though the smokehouse and its wonderful aromas had always been a big temptation to Rex, he gave up on it and followed Nate toward what was once the barn. The dazed boy walked in a kind of disbelieving slow motion.

They reached the barn, or what little was left of the structure. The huge beams that had formed the skeleton of the sturdy building were still standing, but they were charred and still glowing cherry red in places. Nate walked through the rubble, pushing aside charred remains with his shoes. Rex tried to follow, but the ground was too hot for his foot pads so he waited.

Sparks flew up with every crunching step that Nate took. He kicked away a jumbled pile of blackened wood and spotted a shovel face. The handle had burned away, and the metal face was too hot to pick up. Nate wedged the toe of his shoe under the shovel and gave it a mighty kick designed to propel the blade out of the ruins. The projectile did not quite make it.

The blade struck one of the simmering wooden uprights causing a near-lethal chain reaction. Reduced to a frail honeycomb by the flames, the once strong timber snapped and buckled. Rex instantly began barking frenetically, which snapped Nate back into the moment. As the timber fell, the crosspieces above collapsed and crashed toward the ground. Nate bounded out of the way and made a last second dive to safety as all of the beams fell like dominoes. Rex rushed over to Nate, who lay on the ground on his stomach, gasping for breath and looking at the spark-spewing mass that had once been the Chandler barn.

Before he could formulate his thoughts, he heard the sound of hooves on the packed dirt road. Prepared for the worst, he managed to stand. But, it was only a neighbor, Ben Ashby, and his wife and children in their wagon galloping toward him.

"Nate! Nate!" Ashby shouted as he pulled the wagon to a sliding stop. "Are all well?!"

"No. All are not well," Nate said in a monotone. "But they are being tended to and will survive."

"Thank the Lord!" Ashby exclaimed. "Come with us! Williamsburg will offer refuge! The Clarksons and Smythes are already en route there! Mr. Compington says he will stay and fight, but he's a fool!"

"I will not leave," Nate said evenly.

"You must!" Ashby exclaimed. "You see what they are capable of!"

"There is nothing else they can do here," Nate said in a flat voice. "Take your family to safety, but I will not go with you."

Ashby started to argue the point, but his wife touched his arm, and her look stopped further conversation. She could see in Nate's eyes that he needed to stay.

"God watch over you," Mrs. Ashby said softly.

Her husband turned the wagon, and they continued on their way.

Nate began limping away from the burned buildings and across the field where he had been with the oxen. Rex leaned against him as they walked, unwilling not to be in contact with his master. In sharp contrast to the carnage behind them, Nate and Rex walked through a beautiful stand of vividly blooming purple wildflowers as they approached the area where the oxen had been slashed by Adickes. The huge animals were gone.

Nate could tell from the many horse hoofprints and drag marks that the oxen had been towed away by the British. They had probably been fine steak for Tarleton and his bloodthirsty dragoons. Nate noticed an ox harness and the stump chain left on the ground.

Although Nate knew what to expect, he nonetheless started walking up the rise that would offer him a view of the cow pasture below. Rex finally left the boy's side and took point a few feet ahead. The big dog put only a little weight on his right rear leg as he led Nate through more wildflowers. These were bright yellow.

"Oh, Lord," Nate prayed out loud. "Please let there be at least one left."

It was a prayer unanswered. As Nate and Rex topped the rise and looked down, they saw that every single cow was gone. Nate sank dizzily down to the ground. After a few silent moments, he tried to stand, but something was wrong. He could barely straighten up, and his arms and legs were stone heavy. Taking a step was a difficult, slow-motion exercise. His vision became blurry, and the boy thought his neck would surely break from the ever-tightening knot that crept up from his shoulders. As he became completely disoriented and fell back to the ground, he thought that his injuries must be worse than imagined and he was dying.

Then the gate opened. Nate was not immobilized and dying from a physical wound; he was emotionally overwhelmed with what had happened to his family and their home. At first, he sobbed softly; then he held his head in his hands and openly cried. A wail came from his deepest place, and Rex cowered. The tears flowed, and the sobs shook Nate's young body for several minutes until he was cried out. A few more minutes passed. Then Nate stood up, reached down, picked up a round stone, and flung it with all of his might down toward the newly flattened brush trail leading from the pasture and through a destroyed section of fence.

"Burn in Hades!" he yelled at the now deserted route the redcoats had taken with his family's cows. Then he threw another stone, then another.

The herd had been his father's dream. A smart and forward-thinking man, William had figured out that the ever-growing colony of Virginia would inevitably result in an insatiable need for more and more beef.

William and Nate had spent years carefully breeding, nurturing, tending, and birthing their cattle. One more successful calving season, William had said, and Virginians will know that Chandler beef is the best in the colonies. Rachel had contributed very innovative suggestions as how to make sure buyers would get the product in a fresh and economical way. Now, there would be no Chandler beef. Now, Nate thought, there will be no anything.

Rex was a herd dog. His job was to keep the Chandler cattle safe and together. In his own animal way, Rex too felt a gnawing void as he looked at the empty pasture. He paced back and forth, looking.

Nate sat down and called Rex over. He put his arm around the big dog and said, "They're gone, old friend, all gone. But someone will pay for . . . all of this."

Chapter 3

Nate had so much to think about, so much to do, that his mind was numb. Somehow, he felt that, if he kept moving, he could block out some of what had happened and not let the fear of the unknown and the rage building in his throat make him go crazy.

Nate knew he would have to figure out a way to tell his parents everything was gone, but not now. Instead, he and Rex walked to the edge of the woods and down a bank to the creek. They followed it along until they came to the deep pool where the dog and boy had spent many fun times. Ordinarily, Rex would have found a stick and dropped it at Nate's feet for throwing and retrieving, but Rex too was hurt and sensed this was not the time for play.

Nate removed his shoes, stockings, breeches, and the nice but uncomfortably oversized shirt Miss Albright had given him. He waded out into the pool until the cool water was up to his neck. Even though Miss Albright's treatment had helped, the water really soothed his burns. Rex swam out and also felt relief on his burns and cuts. They spent a few minutes gliding through the water, and then Nate washed out his ox blood–stained breeches and hung them on a limb to dry.

There was a big flat rock that jutted out into the pool, and, on the rare occasions when Nate was caught up with his work or sometimes on a Sunday afternoon in the summer, he would lie on the rock and think about things. Rex also liked the smooth surface of the big rock and would peacefully snooze while his master contemplated important subjects.

There were many important subjects to contemplate today. The house, barn, and other outbuildings were all destroyed. Their contents, including stored foodstuffs, were also destroyed. There was not a live chicken, sheep, cow, or horse anywhere. The war had no longer passed his family by. Enough food, a solid roof over their heads, and high expectations for a good future were all destroyed in an insane fifteen minutes. Nate knew his parents faced many long months of recovery, and now everything was on his shoulders. Except for Rex, he would not have felt more alone if he were on the moon.

Nate's body and mind needed rest. His parents were badly hurt, his neighbors had fled, and he could barely function. He put his hands behind his head and looked up through the trees. Rex laid down as close to him as he could get. Nate put a hand on his dog's side and fought to keep his eyes open because he feared what horrible dreams he might have, but he should not have worried about that. Some greater, merciful power cleared his head of the nightmare and allowed the exhausted boy to sleep.

*****

Nate and Rex were jolted wide awake by violent thrashing and the loud snapping of limbs in the woods near the rock where they had been sleeping.

"They're back!" Nate whispered in a frantic voice as he tugged on his clothes and shoes.

He and Rex ran helter-skelter up the stream bank and out into the open by the burned buildings. Nate jerked his head around searching for some kind of weapon. As he negotiated through the still-warm remnants of their house, he stepped on something and hesitated. Nate leaned down and fished Sergeant Adickes's fancy dragoon sword from the coals. The weapon was of the finest hardened steel, and, except for some heat discoloration and a burned-away leather grip, it was perfect, the blade still razor sharp.

"They will kill us," Nate said to Rex, "but not before we take down the murderer who owns this sword!"

With that, Nate and Rex charged back down the hill toward the stream. The crashing and thrashing was still going on somewhere close by. They slipped as silently as Indians through the wooded growth until they were all but on top of the noise.

Nate grasped the sword with both hands, looked into Rex's eyes for a long second, took a deep breath, and, using the long blade, pushed aside a thick branch. There were no dragoons on the other side, but there was one very mad wild pig. The red-eyed, curled-tusk monster was trying its best to kill a black man.

James was a strong man in his early thirties with a neck so thick it seemed to be just a short extension of his wide shoulders. His eyes were dark and penetrating and reflected high intelligence although they were now wide with fear. Short, stocky legs supported his body, which tapered down from the wide shoulders to a narrow waist. He wore coarse linen trousers and a flimsy shirt with full sleeves rolled up to his elbows, and he was barefoot. James was an impressive man but no match for two hundred pounds of enraged feral fury. He was also not a man who was comfortable with the woods and animals. He was not frightened in such settings; he simply did not feel as easy in them as did many rural Virginians.

The beast had James cornered against a blackberry-covered rise. The pig snorted and pawed at the ground, the last exercise before he would stage a slashing, gnawing charge. The man had a slender three-foot-long limb in his hands, but it might as well have been a toothpick.

Nate's natural reaction to help someone in trouble kicked in.

"When my dog starts barking, run!" Nate shouted.

James had spent his entire life on a plantation, so a veritable Noah's ark of animals surrounded him day and night. Knowing how to feed, raise, slaughter, and dress domestic livestock was such an inherent part of plantation life that no one thought of those chores as anything more than routine. There were those, however, who had a natural affinity for animals. James was not one of those people. Perhaps part of the reason was because James had been a house slave since boyhood. His owner, Mr. Armistead, had noticed the youth's intelligence and calm demeanor and rightfully concluded that his talents would be wasted in a tobacco field. Over the years, James had learned all the ins and outs of running a big house and was especially skilled at serving meals in an efficient, proper, and unobtrusive way. None of that prepared him for the rage of a wild boar.

James jerked his head toward Nate and said in a shaky voice, "If I run, he'll drag me down from behind."

"No, he won't!" Nate yelled. "Do it!"

Nate and Rex had both been on wild boar hunts with William. They knew what to do.

"Pig, Rex! Pig!" Nate shouted at Rex.

The dog ran toward the boar barking menacingly.

"Run!" Nate shouted to James.

With no real choice, the man bolted to his right as Rex darted in, out, and around the pig barking like a dog possessed, and the boar turned his livid attention to the new intruder. As Rex had learned on the hunts with William, his job was to get the wild animal cornered. After a minute or so of barking, bobbing, and weaving, he did just that. The wild pig was now in the exact corner where he had pinned the man.

Nate stood behind Rex with the sword drawn back, parallel to the ground.

"Now!" he ordered Rex.

The big dog lunged directly at the face of the pig. As the demonic monster propelled himself at the dog, Rex dropped flat to the ground at the last possible second. The momentum of the pig coincided with the thrust of Nate's sword. The blade passed through the pig's mouth and a foot out of the back of the animal's neck. The wild hog was dead, but the force of the charge had driven the animal on top of Nate, who gagged and gasped for breath under the dead weight.

"By the Almighty!" James said as he ran over and, with a giant effort, rolled the big pig off of Nate. "Are you injured, sir?"

"No, not hurt," Nate coughed.

Rex gave the dead hog one last growl.

James extended his hand to help Nate up, but the teen had a strange reaction to the gesture. He rolled away from the man and jumped to his feet in a combative stance.

"Are you a slave?!" Nate demanded.

"Yes, sir, I am a slave true."

"My father said that, if a slave joined the redcoats, he was a free man."

"Well, sir, I heard sumpin' 'bout that, but I a'n't no . . ."

"You're a British spy!" Nate screamed at the slave.

"No, sir! I . . ."

Nate was not listening. He grabbed the grip of his sword, which protruded from the pig's neck. He tried to pull it out, but the blade was wedged in the dead animal and would not budge. Frantic, Nate gave a mighty tug but slipped and fell down.

The slave grabbed the grip of the sword and, with a powerful yank, snatched it from the pig.

"Give me that sword, you dirty spy!" Nate yelled.

"I a'n't likely givin' a sword to a man with murder in his eyes," James said, locking a strong look on the boy.

He raised the long, curved sword. A trickle of pig blood ran down the frighteningly sharp blade.

Nate's logic and reason were muddled by the previous day's brutality and loss. He leaned down and picked up a jagged piece of stone.

"Then I'll kill you anyway!"

Nate raised the stone above his head and charged.

A ray of sun flashed off of the dragoon sword as it slashed down in a blurlike arc.

Chapter 4

James drove the sword into the ground between himself and Nate. At the same instant, the powerful slave stopped the rock's descent in midair with his other hand.

"Stop!" he shouted. "There a'n't no reason for this!"

"There is a reason!" Nate shouted back. "And you and your kind die for it!"

James pitched the rock aside and held his hands defensively in front of himself. Rex growled, but did not advance.

"You give me one minute," James said. "If you still want to come at me after that, I won't stop you."

James pulled the sword from the ground and handed it, grip first, to Nate. Surprised, Nate grasped the sword grip, and they held a look for a few seconds. Nate finally took a breath.

"One minute," he said and then raised the sword.

James pulled up his pants leg exposing a small canvas bag tied to his calf.

Suspicious, Nate tightened his grip on the sword and ordered, "Don't you try any tricks."

"No tricks, just paper," James said.

Nate took a step back and nodded. James untied the small bag and extracted a folded document.

"Can you read?" he asked.

"My mother taught me to read well and good," Nate said and motioned for James to hand him the paper.

"Watch him, Rex," Nate commanded and then backed up another two steps.

Continuing to cut his eyes up at James, the boy unfolded the document and began to read. He was obviously not a very fast and skilled reader, but he struggled through to the end of it.

"Why would your master, this Mr. Armistead, allow you to go and join the revolutionaries?" Nate asked.

"Because he's a good man, and I seed it as a way to maybe help change sumpin'."

"Change what?"

"I a'n't exactly sure." The big slave looked off into the sky for a moment. "But sometimes it just time to get in the middle of important happnin's."

"You could still become a British spy."

"Well, sir, when there's two sides quarrelin' and fightin', sooner or later, a man mus' pick a side. Now, from what I understand, them redcoats got ships and men and Lord knows what all spread out round the world. To my simple head, whatever they promisin' round here a'n't nothin' to'm. Like a little ant in a big field. On the other hand, to patriots like yoself and Mr. Armistead, this war is everthing. Like a bear in the house. I'm a'thinkin', if change a'comin' out'a it, it'll be for whoever need change the most. That why this James a'n't no redcoat spy."

Nate looked at James for a moment and then, with the sword, indicated the steep stream bank.

"Start up that bank there. Me and my dog'll be right behind you so don't try anything. Go on, now."

As they made their way up the steep bank, James looked over at Nate and said, "Judgin' by your burns and cuts and all, it appear sumpin' bad happen round here."

"Keep moving," Nate said.

"Redcoats?" James asked as he grabbed a small bush to pull himself up the last few feet.

"Stop talking," Nate said.

They made it to the top of the bank, through a line of trees, and out into the open where James saw the destruction for the first time.

"Oh, sweet Jesus," he said, and then to Nate, "Yo home?"

Nate nodded.

"Yo people? Was they in the middle'a . . ."

"My parents are alive," Nate responded instantly and then looked away.

"Praise the Lord! Thank you for yo mercy, Lord," James said as he looked heavenward, and then to Nate, "I mighty sorry for yo loss, young sir."

Nate swallowed hard but said nothing. The point of the sword dropped to the ground, and the fire of distrust in the boy's eyes went out.

Nate got a little dizzy and missed a step.

"You need some food," James said.

"There is no food," Nate responded.

"Oh, there some food," James said.

By sundown, Nate, Rex, and James were sitting by a fire near the stream eating roasted wild pig.

As James held a piece of pork on the end of a stick in the flames, he said, "What you plannin' now?"

"I don't know exactly," Nate said and tossed a piece of meat to Rex. "Kill a man."

"One man don't do nothin'. It what he a part of that caused all this misry."

Nate chewed for a while, thinking, but he stayed quiet.

"Join the army and git to the heart of it."

Nate pulled apart some ribs but said nothing.

"You'll starve out here. You might as well eat army food while you huntin' them redcoats."

Nate chewed the last of some pork from a rib bone.

"You know where to go to enlist?" he asked James.

"Yep."

"Will they give me a musket?"

"Yes, sir. One with a bayonet."

Nate gave the rib bone to Rex and then laid back on the ground.

"We'll see," he said and drifted off to sleep.

When James woke up the next morning, Nate and Rex were gone. The slave thought about looking for them but knew that Nate would have to deal with recent events in his own way. He wished Nate well on his search, but he had his own journey to make. James took one last look around and then began walking west toward the Continental army that he had heard was encamped at a plantation about twenty miles away.

James walked at a steady pace, but, before he got far, Rex trotted up. The dog wagged his tail and gave the slave an obligatory sniff before scouting out the edge of the road. James turned and saw Nate coming down the hill through the wildflowers. The boy carried the ox harness and dragged the stump-pulling chain behind him. He walked in a detached, almost zombielike way.

"And what is this?" James asked as Nate walked up.

"The only things they left," Nate said without emotion. "This is everything my family owns."

James looked at the harness and chain.

"Well, sir, the road can be a surprising place. You never know what might come in handy."

He rolled up the chain and hung it over his shoulder.

"You ready?" he asked Nate.

"Yes," Nate said without enthusiasm.

"How 'bout, you?" James asked Rex.

Rex responded with a bark and wagging tail.

"Let's go."

Nate had made a decision, and he was not looking back. Rex could sense the adventure and bounded ahead sniffing everything in their path. Every few seconds, he would look back to make certain Nate and James were following him along his expertly scouted route.

James soon suggested they move off the road into the stands of trees that ringed most of the open fields.

"Redcoats is swarmin' round here like bees," he explained.

It was a clear, sunny day, and the evergreens smelled good like they always did. It was Nate's favorite place to be, but it also amplified his sadness.

"The smell of these pine trees reminds me of my father," he said with tears welling up in his eyes.

"You hold on to that," James said. "You and yo daddy be walkin' round in the woods again one day."

Nate nodded, wiped at his eyes, and kept walking.

"Um, is yo parents 'round here close?" James asked.

"Close enough," Nate replied.

"Sometime, it a'n't the worst idea in the world to tell the grown people when you 'bout to do sumpin' unusual.

Like in joining up wit the army, sumpin' like that," James said.

"They will understand," Nate said.

He had thought about it all night. He knew that, if his mother begged him not to join the army, he would not. He also knew that, if his father was awake and forbade him to join, he would not. But, Nate was driven to take action against the British, and he was sure he would regret it if he did nothing. No, he would enlist first and then tell them.

"Well, good," James said but did not look convinced.

They kept on walking.

At midday, the trio sat in a shady spot and ate some of the leftover pork. It was a quiet meal. As a slave, James would not ordinarily initiate conversation, and, besides, Nate had a lot to deal with. If there was to be talk, it would start with Nate.

Nate pitched Rex a piece of meat and then drew some random lines in the dirt with a small stick.

He exhaled deeply and said, "My father would have given them the cows, sheep, everything. He would have seen there was no good outcome in fighting such a force."

James nodded at the wisdom of that but didn't say anything.

"Why would soldiers hurt people who aren't soldiers?" Nate asked. His voice began to rise in anger. "Innocent people who bear only meager weapons and show no opposition?"

"War don't make a lot of sense sometimes," James replied. "Mr. Armistead said a lots of it has to do with just makin' people wonder what'll happen next. He said, when you beat a man in his head, there a'n't no more need for musket balls."

Nate snapped his drawing stick, and there was fire in his eyes.

"There will be musket balls," he shot back. "A plenty of them."

"I a'n't a'doubtin' that, sir," James said.

Nate flopped back and looked up through the green branches at the sun for a few minutes and then asked, "After we beat them, what will you do then?"

"Well, see, that right there's what I a'n't got no idea about. I'm a slave, and I reckon a thinkin' man would say I'd best not be expectin' no big difference, but, somehow or other, I do. The patriots are fightin' to be free, and I guess somewhere's down deep so'm I."

"So you think this war will set you free?"

"Oh, not me more'n likely, but I'm thinkin' one kind'a freedom might one day spread on out to another and one more and then, down the road a ways, people will just be people and that'll be that."

Before Nate could respond, Rex jumped up growling, ears and eyes on high alert. Nate held up a hand to Rex to be quiet, and then they all crept silently through the trees to a spot where they could look out at the road.

Two regular British cavalrymen—one quite tall, the other an average-sized man with flaming red hair—rode along trying to keep a small herd of cattle together. They were not very good at it. A farmer followed. His hands were tied behind him and another length of rope was around his neck. The other end of the rope was looped over the neck of the tall man's horse and ran under the rider's left leg. The farmer was forced to shuffle along behind the two horses and his stolen cattle.

"They're doing to that man what their comrades did to my family," Nate whispered in a chillingly angry tone as he physically restrained Rex, who was dying to go herd the cattle.

"Leave it be," James whispered back. "There a'n't nothin' we can do."

"That man will have his cattle back, and he will live," Nate spit through clenched teeth.

"Oh, Lord," James said, but he followed Nate back to their lunch spot and the ox harness and chain, which were in a heap on the ground.

Although moving along at an unhurried pace, the regular British cavalrymen still had a problem keeping the small herd of twelve cattle together. There was too much temptation in the form of fresh tall grass, clover, and other treats along the side of the road for the hungry cattle to resist.

"Bloody cows," the redheaded man said. "We should just shoot them right here and let the supply unit carry them off."

"No!" the farmer yelled.

"We should surely shoot this annoying farmer," the tall man said.

"Go ahead, you thieving plunderers!" the farmer managed to shout before the tall man gave his horse a slight spur, and the rope tightened against the prisoner's windpipe again.

"We'll leave killing at random to Colonel Tarleton and his lunatic dragoons," the redhead responded. "We take prisoners like proper English soldiers."

The furious farmer could not let it go: "There's nothing proper at all about stealing a man's . . ."

Before he could finish, Rex streaked out of the trees straight for the scattered herd and started doing what he did best, herding. The cavalrymen were not sure what was going on, but it was certainly working, and they did not see any advantage to interfering. In only a couple of minutes, Rex had the herd nicely grouped and moving along together.

"Now, sir, that is a dog we could use," the tall man said.

"Hear, hear," enthused the redhead. "Throw him some meat else he might run off."

At that moment, Nate walked out onto the road from a narrow pig trail that angled off of the main road and into a line of trees that separated two large plantations. He held a six-foot-long stick that he raised high in the air.

"What's this lad doing, then?" the tall cavalryman asked.

It became obvious that second. Nate pointed the stick toward the trail. Rex saw the signal and hustled the cows off the road and onto the narrow path. The big animals had to go single file, but Rex and Nate kept them in queue and moving swiftly.

"Stop that! Stop there!" the redheaded soldier barked. "Those cows are property of His Majesty the King!"

"Like hell!" the farmer shouted. "Go, girls! Run for your lives!" he yelled after his cows.

The last cow disappeared down the pig trail and so did Nate and Rex. The horsemen spurred their mounts toward the narrow opening. The farmer tried to run at full speed to keep up, but it was hopeless. He fell and was being dragged first along the road and then into the narrow confines of the shadowy trail. The rope around his thick neck was, at that point, a hangman's noose, and the farmer was seconds away from suffocation, a broken neck, or both.

Then the rope went slack, and the British cavalrymen went sailing up into space, did a nice midair turn, and slammed onto the ground. Nate had cut the rope with one slash of his dragoon sword. Gagging and gasping for air, the farmer rose to his knees and saw Nate and James unhurriedly tying the unconscious soldiers to a tree with the ox harness. The chain was stretched across the trail about mounted-British-cavalryman high.

After a short period, Rex had the twelve cows and the two cavalry horses in a manageable huddle. Nate exchanged the comically large shirt Miss Albright had given him for the fine one he had removed from the redheaded man, a perfect fit. The tall man's scabbard was not dragoon style, but it was serviceable for Sergeant Adickes's sword. The reins were tight around the redcoats and the tree, but James added gags just to make sure the boys didn't wake up, raise a ruckus, and get rescued before everyone made a clean getaway.

Although his voice was just a raspy whisper thanks to the rope injuries, the farmer put a hand on Nate's shoulders and said, "You boys saved the only two things I got left in my life; my life itself and them cows. I thank you and I thank the good Lord for sending you my way. You boys is angels, and I must thank you in some way."

"No. Just . . . tend well to your cattle," Nate said after a moment of thought.

"Ah, but I had fences and good pasture now laid waste by the redcoats."

"Hmm," James said to Nate. "You know about a pasture wit only a little broke fence somewhere's 'round here? I'm just askin'."

Nate got the hint.

"About eight miles down the road, you'll come across a big turtle shell next to a farm trail," he said. "Run your cattle in there. The farm you'll come to is gone, but, up and over the hill covered with flowers, you'll find a good, fenced pasture, and the British won't be back to it. Use it as long as you need."

"I am deeply in your debt," the farmer replied gratefully and looked over at the two cavalry mounts. "Although they are not mine to give, perhaps those two horses will be some recompense for your bravery."

"I don't need no horse," James said quickly. "Where we goin', I'm better off walkin'."

Nate could hear his father's voice saying that stealing was stealing, and taking the British horses did not feel right.

"Take both of them," he said to the farmer. "If he's walking, I'm walking."

And walk they did. By early evening, James was certain they were within a couple of miles of William Tyree's plantation where he had heard the American soldiers were camped. The increased traffic on the road seemed to confirm that they were near the end of their trek. Supply wagons, cannons pulled by horse teams, camp followers, soldiers, and locals infused the area with energy. Nate took it all in, but his mind processed everything through the still-dazed filter of what had happened to his parents and home. What should have been an exciting scene was, to him, just so much hazy motion. He was surprised, however, by the number of slaves he saw on the road and in the adjacent fields.

"I should have thought most slaves would be off with the British," he said.

"Oh, some'a these people you see 'round here will go to the redcoats directly. One reason's cause now there's some redcoats 'round here to go to."

"Pardon?"

"A royal guv'ner can say a rebel's slave be free if he join up wit the British, but, till recent, there a'n't been many redcoats near to join up wit. Before Cornwallis and them boys got close, a slave'd be in for a long hard trip was he to jest strike out lookin' for a pack'a English to take him in. Besides, there's more to it."

"What would that be?"

"See, bein' a slave a'n't no good way to live, but, when a man leave it to join up wit the British army somewhere or other, he leavin' more'n jest bein' a slave."

"What else does he leave?"

"Family and, more'n likely, the only home he ever known. A'n't two more things much stronger to a man."

Nate nodded. Winter flashed through his mind. He had always felt safe and loved in the family's home, but, in the spring, summer, and early fall, the days were long and there was so much to do that the three of them did little inside but eat and sleep. When winter came, however, daylight was short-lived, and the family spent many hours together in the warm house. After supper, his father sat by the fire and repaired tools or whittled while Nate and Rachel took turns reading aloud. The Chandlers owned just three books: the Bible, the Book of Common Prayer, and the cumbersomely titled *A New History of England; from the Invasion of Julius Caesar to the End of George 11d. Adorned with Cuts of All Kings and Queens Who Have Reigned Since the Norman Conquest.* While some of the Bible stories could stir Nate's adventurous spirit, it was *A New History* that set his dreams a flight. The book was filled with gallantry, heroes, and strategy.

"Also, like I said before, some'a this freedom talk have a good, strong ring to it."

Nate walked a few more steps, thinking, and then said, "It all seems complicated."

"Yep."

After walking a bit farther, James needed to relieve himself so Nate and Rex sat down to watch the road action and wait on their companion. And they waited. Too much time passed, and Nate wondered what was keeping James. Rex led Nate along the edge of the busy road as they looked for the slave. No luck, so Nate was about to go down in the trees to look for him when he heard a loud and desperate, "Nate!"

James was shackled in the back of a wagon. A huge man in a wide black hat and long dark cloak was driving the rig. The giant's whip came down, and the horses broke into a trot. Nate and Rex ran through the road traffic after the giant, his wagon, and their new friend.

Chapter 5

The huge man's wagon was slowed by some traffic, enabling Rex and Nate to catch up. The boy was certainly scared, but something came over him as he approached the wagon. Some combination of impending conflict and adrenalin put his nerves on high alert, but he also felt surprisingly calm. As Nate walked by James, the boy gave the chained-up slave a reassuring, confident wink.

Nate grabbed one of the horse's bridles.

"Stop this wagon immediately, sir!" he snapped with authority at the enormous driver.

The man had an incredibly thick black beard and inky eyes so deeply set in his head that they could not be seen in the shadow of the wide hat. His calloused, scarred hands were so big that just one of them could have encased Nate's head in a death grip.

The giant looked down at Nate with no more interest than he would have given an annoying mosquito.

"You remove your hand from my horse," the huge man said. His voice sounded like a bass drum.

"Gladly, sir," Nate responded looking the giant right in the eye. "Just as soon as you unchain this man."

"This man is a runaway slave, and he's going back to his owner in Gloucester."

"Pardon me for saying so, sir, but I believe you've made quite a mistake. This man has a pass."

"He's goin' to Gloucester, and I then get my bounty. I don't care about no papers, and I don't care about you."

With that, the gigantic man brought his whip down on the horses, and the wagon lurched away. The action pulled Nate's hand from the bridle, but he ran alongside as the horses were whipped into a fast trot.

"If I were you, I would not count on going all the way to Gloucester!" he yelled up at the driver, who responded by slapping the whip across Nate's chest and knocking him to the ground.

"Who'll stop me?" the massive man laughed as he forced the horses into a gallop. "You?"

In the back of the fast-moving wagon, James looked frantic as he yanked at his chains. Nate pulled himself up, and he and Rex ran after the rolling prison, which scattered pedestrians and carts alike as it rounded a sharp curve near a shallow stream. Gasping for breath, Nate was losing sight of the wagon and knew he would never catch it on the road. He put his hands on his knees and sucked in air as it disappeared behind a line of trees. Although he had known the slave for only two days, there was something reassuring about the black man's presence, and Nate was not ready for another loss in his life.

"Come back!" he screamed. "Come back!"

"He will not be coming back," an elderly man shepherding six sheep along the road said to Nate, "nor, may I say, will you be catching him."

"But that man should not be in irons! He has permission from . . ."

"At least, you will not catch such strong horses by following the road. Of course, following the road is not always the best path."

"I fail to understand, sir."

The elderly man pointed out across a sloped field. From their higher vantage point, Nate could see that the road all but doubled back on itself as it wound along following the stream's meandering path. If he ran through the field in a straight line, he just might intercept the bounty hunter, but it would be close.

"My gratitude, sir," he thanked the elderly man and was off with Rex close behind.

The downhill grade made it easier to maintain top speed. A few rotting tree stumps were hurdled, and, breathless, they finally reached the road. Nate saw soldiers, carts, farmers, and slaves but not the wagon.

Nate reasoned that, if he waited at that spot and the wagon had already passed, he would lose it forever. It made the most sense to continue on. He proceeded at a trot along the edge of the road.

Around a bend, four American soldiers and a Captain Rawlinson were helping a thin woman and her five children with their oxcart. The rickety, two-wheeled conveyance that appeared to carry all of the family's possessions had bogged down in a rivulet that had washed over the dirt road. The cart was at a precarious angle, and the soldiers had unhitched the ox. The massive animal stood calmly in the middle of the road as the soldiers unloaded the heavier items from the cart.

Nate approached the young, handsome Rawlinson, who had removed his tunic and hat and was working alongside his men.

"My apologies, sir, but have you per chance seen a wagon driven by a large man wearing a wide hat and carrying a slave in chains pass this way?" Nate asked.

"I think not," Rawlinson said and lifted a heavy trunk from the cart. "And I would most certainly have noticed such a spectacle."

He lowered the trunk to the ground and said to his men, "Let's give it a try, lads. I think we can lift it now. Especially since we have the added shoulder of this skinny, but sturdy enough, farm lad."

The soldiers put their shoulders under the edge of the cart, and, responding to Rawlinson's hand gesture, Nate did the same.

"Heave and step!" the captain ordered. "Heave!"

The cart almost rolled free, but there was not quite enough manpower. Rawlinson bent his knees and added his own broad shoulders to the task.

"Once more, boys! Heave! Heave and step!"

The captain rose up with the others. After much grunting and pushing, the cart rolled out of the gully. The soldiers and five children cheered.

"Oh, thank you, sirs. Thank you!" the weary mother said.

"Not at all, madam," Rawlinson said with a slight bow. "Reload this woman's possessions," he directed his men, and to Nate, "Perhaps you would be so kind as to hitch up her ox."

"I . . . yes, sir, but . . ."

Nate saw that the bounty hunter's wagon had arrived during the cart excavation and was in line waiting for the road to be cleared. Without a word, Nate walked away from the captain.

"See here!" the annoyed captain said.

There was no time to think. Nate took a breath and walked down the line.

The bounty hunter squinted under his wide hat and said, "You once more. This time, 'twill be a bloody lesson you learn."

He raised the whip.

Nate looked unconcerned and said evenly, "I fear you are the one facing an unpleasant situation. You see, when Mr. Jefferson learns that his favorite house slave has been carted away to Gloucester, I suspect Mr. Jefferson will send out word to various friends and military men that Gloucester is not where he wants his favorite house slave to be."

"Jefferson?"

"Yes, sir, the man you have chained up there knows Mr. Thomas Jefferson's needs almost as well as the distinguished man knows them himself. Being the saddle boy for the esteemed Mr. Jefferson, I can tell you that he relies on this man many times a day."

"Thomas Jefferson?"

"So, the way I see it, I can run right down the road to where Mr. Thomas Jefferson is currently conducting some business and tell him that a very large man in a wide hat and a long cloak driving a wagon pulled by two bays with white forelegs has taken his favorite man to Gloucester. About then, I suspect he will make some arrangements that might well prevent you from claiming your bounty."

The giant glared down at Nate, who shrugged.

"Or you could just unchain this man and be on your way."

Although Nate was intimidated by the man's immense size and threatening posture, he did not show it and held a steady look with the leviathan.

A few moments of terrifying silence from the big man, and then he turned in his seat and reached back for James. He snatched the slave up to him, unlocked the chains, and threw him to the ground as if James weighed no more than a small child. The whip came down on the horses, and the wagon and the giant plowed through the scattering crowd and away.

Nate helped James up, and they followed Rex over to the side of the road and sat down. Both were shaking and neither said anything for a short while. Then, James began to chuckle.

"Thomas Jefferson?" he said with a shake of his head and laughed.

There was a trace of sparkle in his eyes as Nate said, "It seemed like a good idea at the time."

He cut a look over at James and did something he had not done since the attack on the farm. He smiled.

Nate looked up and right into the eyes of Captain Rawlinson.

"Sir," Nate jumped up. "I apologize about the ox, sir, but . . ."

"Why, not at all," Captain Rawlinson said with a twinkle in his eye. "Thomas Jefferson's saddle boy must have many important matters to attend. And how, pray tell, is Mr. Jefferson? In good health and fine disposition, I trust."

Nate and James cut each other a concerned look.

"Uh . . ."

"I see him often at the Eagle Tavern. I'll be sure to tell him I have met the two most treasured members of his household."

"Um, sir," Nate said nervously, "we don't really work

for Mr. Jefferson, but, you see, James here has permission to . . ."

Captain Rawlinson laughed. James and Nate looked at each other, confused.

"It was quite a brilliant performance if I may say."

"It was?"

"Yes, indeed. Very quick thinking. The army could use such sharp wit and bravery."

James and Nate exhaled with relief.

"That's where we're going," Nate said and pulled back his shoulders. "To enlist."

"Good. Follow me, then," Captain Rawlinson said and mounted his horse.

Nate, James, and Rex moved out into the road activity and trotted to keep up with the young officer and his men.

They came to Tyree's plantation only a mile further down the road. Hundreds of military tents dotted the grounds. Horses, cattle, and other livestock were being tended by soldiers and slaves. Groups of soldiers huddled and talked of war. Other soldiers drilled or received instruction on artillery weapons. The big plantation house itself was being used as a temporary headquarters, and a steady stream of officers and enlisted men went in and out of the attractive white structure. Nate and James could feel their anticipation rise as they looked at the busy, exciting scene.

Captain Rawlinson told James and Nate that it would be the next morning before he would finish his reports and could discuss their enlistment. A private took them to a cooking pit and made sure they were fed. While they sat cross-legged on the ground and ate, they listened to some of the veteran soldiers talk of their military exploits in New York. Nate and James slept on the ground, and the boy dreamed of his parents and the upcoming battles that would avenge his family's losses.

The next morning, Nate and James waited in front of the house until Captain Rawlinson was ready to see them. Rex kept a steady eye on the cattle that were in a nearby fenced area. Two officers were sitting at a makeshift table playing a game of cards. James and Nate watched as the two men placed wagers, drew cards, and made their final bets. Both men were a second away from showing their hands when a cow mooed and Rex spun toward the sound. As he whipped around, the big dog's tail swept across the table with the efficiency of a good broom. All of the cards on the table and in the men's hands went flying.

"Blast!" one of the officers shouted. "That was a winning hand sure!"

"Ha!" countered the other. "I was holding the hand of a lifetime! Bloody dog!"

"Queen, jack, ten of clubs, nine, eight of spades," James said to the first officer, who looked surprised. "Two and three of spades discarded."

"A three and five of clubs, nine of diamonds, six and eight of hearts," he said to the other. "Ace of clubs, spade queen discarded."

"Nothing!" the first officer exclaimed. "You were bluffing!"

The other officer smiled and said, "Ah, but who is to say you would not have fallen for my ploy? I suppose now we shall never know."

The two officers looked at James with amazement.

"How did you do that?" one of them asked.

"Not sure, sir," James responded. "I kind'a see things in my head, and there they stay."

"You two come with me," the other officer said and indicated the front door of the house. "Not the dog," he continued. "That animal cost me money."

As they entered the house, Captain Rawlinson was coming out of a parlor room being used as a command office.

"Ah, there you are," the captain said to Nate and James. "Leave this to me, lieutenant," he continued to the officer.

Indicating James, the lieutenant said, "Sir, this man has a truly remarkable memory. He remembered every card dealt in a game of chance. Extraordinary, actually."

"Truly?" Rawlinson responded and motioned for Nate and James to follow him into the parlor.

The captain first interviewed Nate and learned of the injuries to his parents and destruction of the farm. The boy was obviously smart and brave, but Rawlinson had some concern about the hatred in Nate's eyes. Of course, channeled properly, that could be an asset and certainly took away any doubt about his loyalty.

"You look mighty young," the captain said.

"I'm damn well old enough to shoot a musket and drive home a bayonet!" Nate overreacted.

Captain Rawlinson raised an eyebrow at the disrespectful tone.

Nate exhaled.

"My apologies, sir," he said and rubbed his temples.

"You've been through quite a lot for a young man," Rawlinson said evenly. "Apology accepted. Besides, you misunderstand. Looking young and harmless would make you a great asset as a courier. Armies run on accurate and timely information. Getting the information through hostile territory and, often, enemy lines requires a cool head, great courage, and, to the point, the ability to be completely inconspicuous."

A private holding some papers tapped at the door.

"A moment," Rawlinson said and stepped from the room.

"I want to fight," Nate said and looked over at James. "You know why I must fight."

"Fightin' a'n't really it. You want revenge and justice," James said. "'Course, if a man was to be smart about it, he'd see takin' out two hundred soldiers with a good piece'a information beat takin' out one man with a bayonet all over the place. But that's just me talkin'."

Narrowing his eyes, Nate stared at the floor and gave that some thought.

*****

Obeying Nate's command to stay outside, Rex sat watching the cows. Hannah, the eight-year-old daughter of the plantation owner, came running around the corner of the house with her hoop and stick. She stopped when she saw Rex.

"My, what a big dog!" she giggled.

Rex wagged his tail and nuzzled her leg when she rubbed his ears.

"Wanna play?" she asked.

Hannah gave the hoop a stroke with the stick, and the circle rolled away at a fast clip.

"Come on!" Hannah said to Rex, and they both took off running after the hoop.

The hoop was rolling down an incline toward the woods and gaining speed. Rex caught up to the runaway hoop and sped along beside it, barking.

"Don't let it get away!" Hannah shouted as she ran as hard as she could to catch up.

The ground sloped away steeply now, and the hoop was really moving. Somehow, it missed several trees in a wooded area near a ravine and rocketed along until it reached a ledge and went airborne. It bounced off a downed tree trunk and rolled down a steep bank into an overgrown dry creek bed. At last, the ring came to a stop. Rex had continued his hot pursuit and came thrashing down the bank through the heavy foliage. Hannah was far behind but continued the chase as best she could.

Rex sniffed at the hoop, took it in his jaws, and started back up the ravine when he suddenly stopped, dropped the hoop, and growled. The hair on his back went straight up, and his ears cocked forward. He stood dead still for a couple of seconds and then took off running down the creek bed through a mass of vines and underbrush and around a bend.

Sergeant Adickes and two of his men were creeping out of the trees toward their hidden horses. The dragoon's scent triggered danger and threat, and, instinctively, Rex attacked Adickes. The assault was savage and meant to kill. The sergeant screamed as he went down but got his arm in front of his throat, which saved him from a quick death. Before the other dragoons could even react, Rex sunk his big teeth into the sergeant's shoulder and began shaking him violently.

"Help! Help! Ye bloody idiots!" Adickes yelled at his men as Rex began dragging him away.

There was too much flailing around to risk a shot or sword thrust, so one of the men started kicking Rex with all of his might. The other one had the courage to actually throw himself on the huge dog from behind and clench his arms around the animal's powerful, thick neck. The lack of air slowed the attack and allowed the three soldiers to finally get Rex immobilized. While the two cavalrymen held him down, Sergeant Adickes hog-tied the dog with his belt and muzzled him with a length of his now ripped and bloody tunic.

Gasping for breath, the three men looked down at Rex, who was straining against his restraints and trying to gnaw through the muzzle. One of the men handed Adickes his dagger expecting the sergeant to kill the dog immediately.

Instead, Sergeant Adickes glared down at Rex and said, "There be no easy death for a devil beast attacking me." He leaned down close to Rex's snarling face. "You'll rue the day you sank your teeth into Clinton Adickes."

Rex lunged at him through the muzzle but could do no harm.

Halfway down the ravine, Hannah was peeking out from behind a tree. Her eyes were wide as she watched the three cavalrymen disappear into the trees. Rex was across the back of Sergeant Adickes's horse.

Chapter 6

"I understand your desire to fight," Captain Rawlinson said after returning to the room, "but your greatest contribution would be as a courier."

Nate looked disappointed. "I have a good sword," he said. "If I had a musket, I could . . ."

Captain Rawlinson was getting annoyed.

"I must talk to this man," he said, indicating James. "Go outside and weigh what has been said here."

"But, I . . . yes, sir."

Nate went outside to think about his choices. He didn't see Rex but figured he was with the cows. As he walked down the steps, a breathless Hannah came running up.

"Mean men are in the woods!" she screamed.

Nate and several soldiers gathered around her.

"You're fine now," Nate reassured her as he kneeled down. "What happened?"

"They took the big dog!"

"What?"

"The mean men beat the dog I was playing with and took him away!"

"What did the men look like?" a tall soldier asked.

"One of them looked like a . . . like a . . . rat!" Hannah said in a rush. "A rat in a green coat, and the big dog was fighting with him, and then the other bad men kicked the doggie and got him all tied up, and then they put him on the horse behind the rat man and they rode away!"

"A big gold dog?" Nate asked, afraid of the answer.

"Yes! With floppy ears and blue eyes like my cousin Anne's!"

"Cursed British! Crawling around in the woods like the vermin they be," a bearded soldier fumed.

"Where would they take the dog?" Nate asked, his jaw in a knot.

"I understand Cornwallis has moved his entire army down to Jamestown," the tall soldier said.

"I need a horse," Nate said to no one in particular and ran back up the steps.

James was crossing the entry hall when Nate ran through the front door.

"What got you all stirred up?" the slave asked.

In his panic, Nate ignored James and pushed into Rawlinson's office.

"Sir, I . . ."

Captain Rawlinson looked up, clearly annoyed at Nate's lack of respect. James shook his head and went outside to wait to hear what had happened.

It was one of those rare times when fate and necessity collided. Nate was going to plead with Captain Rawlinson for a horse he could ride to Jamestown to look for Rex, but he was spared the effort. In the short time Nate and James had been in the camp, critical information had been received that needed to be rushed to General Lafayette, who was en route to Jamestown and a possible conflict with Cornwallis and the British troops.

"Sir, I . . . ," Nate began.

"No more talk of uniforms, muskets, and bayonets," the captain said sternly to Nate. "This packet of information will be delivered safely to General Lafayette, and you, young sir, will be doing the delivering."

"But, my dog . . ."

"Silence!" Rawlinson commanded. "Sergeant Harrington will get you outfitted, and then you will be on your way to Jamestown. Understood?"

"Jamestown?" Nate gave a quick prayer of thanks. "I understand, sir."

Within half an hour, burly Sergeant Harrington had helped Nate prepare. A thin packet clasped with a wax seal hung under his shirt. On a military map, Harrington had shown Nate the route to Jamestown and the most likely spot to find General Lafayette or at least his senior staff. Nate was not to give the packet to anyone under the rank of major. Sergeant Harrington had also shown Nate examples of epaulets and insignia that indicated high-ranking officers.

Then Nate was taken to his horse, Milk. The animal was not the sleek cavalry mount Nate had pictured in his mind but was, rather, a huge, light-colored draft horse.

"Nobody pays much mind to a young lad on a farm horse," the sergeant said.

"But what if I have to gallop or . . ." Nate, agitated, was still thinking about Rex.

"Oh, Milk'll gallop along fine if he has to," Sergeant Harrington said and hoisted Nate up onto the broad bare back. "Off with you, now. Godspeed, boy."

Nate rode over to James and gave him the short version of the situation, bade his friend good-bye, and moved through the camp and onto the road. The big horse had a smooth gait, and sitting on his wide back was like riding along in a comfortable chair. They did not break any speed records, but Milk's even pace put them in Williamsburg around noon. After passing through the city, it would be about seven miles to Jamestown.

Since Cornwallis and the British forces had left Williamsburg a day earlier, there was a good-natured air on the city streets, but there were also some unpleasant leftovers. While Nate waited for an overturned cart to be cleared, he heard a well-dressed man say to his companion, "Among the many plagues the British left us in Williamsburg, that of these flies is the worst. It is impossible to eat, drink, sleep, write, sit still, or even walk about in peace on account of their confounded stings."

His friend replied, "Indeed. Their numbers exceed description, unless you look into the eighth chapter of Exodus for it."

To further cement their unwelcome status, the British forces had commandeered much of the city's food, goods, livestock, and feed. The Continental army was gathering up whatever was left for its own needs, but at least the Americans left IOUs that might have a chance of one day being honored.

Additionally, there were mountains of debris and trash left by the British and an overwhelming amount of manure left by their livestock baking in the July sun. Even though much the same was expected from the Continental troops, and it appeared that normalcy would be a while in coming, there was still much celebrating and jovial activity. Nate was in too big a hurry to slow down and watch. As he and Milk turned south on the road to Jamestown, almost all of the meager traffic was going the other way toward Williamsburg. Apparently, the small number of residents did not want to be caught up in a battle between Lord Cornwallis and General Lafayette.

Milk's plodding pace put them in the Jamestown area by early afternoon. They crossed a narrow bridge over a stream that flowed over a sandy area before eventually emptying into the James River. They continued along the road and then, following Sergeant Harrington's instructions, turned right at a fork in the road that would take them across once-farmed fields that now sat idle toward Green Spring plantation and Lafayette. The sounds of horses, barked orders, and wagons filtered through the air from somewhere close, and Nate became increasingly excited with each thud of Milk's huge hooves on the hard-packed trail.

A still marsh, much larger than the ones near the Chandler farm, snaked its way inland through fields and woods. Some of the swampy terrain was made up of large patches of wet, dark mud so deep that no horse could have trudged through.

"Halt and identify yourself!" rang out and Nate nearly dropped the reins in surprise.

A young American soldier, Jacob Clarke, stepped from behind a small clump of trees at the edge of the marsh. The eighteen-year-old seemed unsure of himself but tried to cover his newness to the task with bluster.

Bluster was one of the reasons not many people liked Clarke. He was too loud, often inappropriate, and always seemed to be trying too hard. As the thirteenth of fourteen children born to a modest brickmaker, he had to make some noise to be noticed, but it was more than that. People who talked to the boy always came away with the impression that Clarke was not really listening and was always trying to somehow "get" something from the other person. He was also a dreamer and had no interest in hard work. His annoying personality and laziness doomed his half-hearted apprenticeship with a Williamsburg saddlemaker. The tradesman released Clarke from his agreement after only a month. In the two years since that failure, the boy had washed out as a barkeep in the Raleigh Tavern and even lost a menial job sweeping the streets. Although Clarke had no military inclinations, joining the Continental army was his last gasp, and at least he was being fed and had a captive audience for his self-serving ramblings in his fellow soldiers. He did notice, however, that he was frequently sent out to sentry posts alone.

Clarke seemed relieved that the intruder was a harmless farm boy.

"This is soon to be a battlefield," the soldier said with great self-importance. "Be off with you, boy!"

"I have an urgent message for General Lafayette," Nate said authoritatively.

"Ha! I can just imagine."

Nate reached up under his shirt.

"Hold on there!" the infantryman said and clumsily leveled his new musket at Nate.

"It's only papers," Nate said and held up the wax-sealed packet. "As a veteran soldier, I'm sure you recognize the official seal."

The soldier squinted up at the packet and said, "Yes, of course, I recognize it." He did not. "General Lafayette, you say?"

Nate nodded.

"This must be personally delivered to the general."

Aha! thought Clarke. His mind raced with the possibilities. He would dismiss this boy and then take the papers to Lafayette himself. He would concoct a story about how cleverly he had obtained the documents, and the general would surely see his potential and promote him on the spot. No years of anonymous drudgery for Jacob Clarke! He could picture himself next to the general during great military campaigns and ceremonies. That will certainly show everyone how important I am and relieve me of this day-to-day military drudgery.

"Give me the documents. I'll deliver them," Clarke said.

"No. I was told to put this packet into the hands of General Lafayette or one of his colonels. That's quite a smart uniform, but I do not see any colonel epaulets, and I am reasonably sure you are not a French general."

He's just like the rest of them! Clarke seethed inside. No respect. He did not intend to spend the length of the war drilling, digging trenches, submitting to orders, and, worst of all, going unnoticed.

"A mouthy lad! Give me that packet!" Clarke demanded and reached out his hand.

"What is your name?" Nate asked calmly.

"Jacob Clarke. Not that my name is any of your . . ."

Nate leveled the same strong, confident look that he had used on the bounty hunter at the nervous private.

"Shall I tell command that Private Jacob Clarke was helpful to the mission or shall I tell them that General Lafayette did not get the information in a timely way because Private Jacob Clarke stood in the way?"

Private Clarke swallowed hard and said, "Give me that packet and be on your way or I will . . . I will . . . arrest you."

Perspiration popped out on Clarke's lip, and he was nervously shifting from foot to foot.

There was no logical reason to explain how Nate could read sneaky or self-serving people. The Chandler farm neighbors were straightforward people. He saw few strangers, and the other people in his life were honest, hard-working friends. Even when the family went to Williamsburg, there was not much interaction on a personal level, just business talk with shopkeepers and tradesmen and idle conversation with people at the market or on the streets. By all rights, Nate should have been naive about people and their motives, and, yet, he knew he had Jacob. Nate had never played a hand of cards, but he would have been very good at it.

"Yes, by all means, arrest me if that will speed up the delivery of this document to General Lafayette," Nate said in an almost-friendly way. "Why, that will do just fine. You tell your tale, and I will, in turn, tell mine. Then, one of us will wait out the battle in irons and disgrace while the other shares in the glory."

Jacob wiped at his now profusely sweating brow and said, "Cease talking!"

Ignoring the order, Nate continued, "Or I could deliver the papers as instructed and tell one and all that Private Clarke steered me down the right path and was instrumental in the success of the mission." Nate hesitated just the right amount of time and then said, "You have the musket. The decision rests with you."

"I . . . you would speak of my help in this matter?"

"Indeed! Your diligence would be most enthusiastically noted."

"I . . . well . . . I have your word?"

"Yes."

Jacob took a last look at the packet, lowered the musket, and said, "You may pass."

"Thank you, sir."

Nate nodded and rode away. Although he knew it was an unlikely place to look, he kept an eye out for Rex. In less than two miles, another sentry, a weathered veteran, stopped Nate by a man-made causeway that spanned a swampy area. The raised earthen and stone mound had a flat top and served as a road across the water and mud. On the other side of the causeway, Nate could see the activity surrounding Lafayette's main force of several thousand men. It was all very exciting.

"A message for General Lafayette," Nate said, trying hard not to sound too important.

The sentry looked at the wax seal and said, "He passed here some time ago with some officers. Down that way, I suspect," and pointed toward the horizon and wooded riverbank two or three miles in the distance.

"The sentry back down the road said this was soon to be a battlefield," Nate said and, remembering his promise, added, "The sentry, Private Clarke, was most helpful."

"Generally speaking, if Clarke's lips are moving, he is spinning a tale," the soldier said with a grin. "But, in this case, he is correct. Cornwallis has moved his main army across the river, but the few hundred men he left as rear guard are about to get a beating they will not soon forget."

"Good!" Nate smiled and saluted.

The amused soldier returned the salute, and Nate rode away.

Nate and Milk angled away from the swamp and loped across woodsy land and open fields. After two miles, they rode up to eight hundred American troops preparing for battle under the watchful eye of General "Mad Anthony" Wayne. There was tension on the soldier's faces but also a sense of barely contained excitement over the combat they all knew was coming soon. No one paid Nate and Milk much attention, but a young lieutenant confirmed that Lafayette and some senior officers were having a meeting near the riverbank a mile or so further on.

It was a few minutes before they reached a rise and Nate could look down and see the river. Toward the rear of an open area ringed with trees, he spotted a man on a glistening coal black Thoroughbred horse. Nate thought that he had never seen a more beautiful animal and concluded that only a general could be worthy of such a magnificent mount. He was right.

The three officers gathered around General Lafayette were given instructions, and they galloped away. Lafayette took the rare moment alone for some deep thought. Nate was hesitant to disturb the general, but he had his orders. As he rode Milk across the cleared area and closer to Lafayette, he was surprised to see that the general was young, probably only a few years older than the nervous private who had first stopped him on the road. Any similarities between those two men ended at age.

Marie-Joseph-Paul-Yves-Roch-Gilbert du Motier, marquis de Lafayette, was born to an aristocratic French family in 1757. His father was killed at the battle of Minden in 1759. Eleven years later, both his mother and grandfather died, leaving the thirteen-year-old orphan a fortune. Following in his father's footsteps, the boy entered the French army at the age of fourteen. He was a captain at nineteen when the British colonies in America proclaimed their independence, and that quest for freedom deeply stirred the young soldier. He would later write in his memoirs that "my heart was enrolled in it."

The marquis de Lafayette had the aura of leadership. There was something indefinable about his carriage, confidence, and bearing that set him apart. Even had he been riding a mule and wearing homespun instead of sitting astride the beautiful black horse uniformed in perfectly tailored finery, men would have followed him into battle. General Lafayette's strength lay in charisma, not props.

However, his initial arrival in America with eleven companions on a boat he had purchased and outfitted himself was not greeted with much enthusiasm by the American Congress. Why should a rich, nineteen-year-old Frenchman be given a commission as a major general as he requested when there were more deserving American officers? Lafayette won them over with his offer to receive no pay, act solely as a volunteer, and finance his troops from his own pocket.

"Pardon, general, sir," Nate said as he rode up.

Lafayette came out of his thought and said, "Yes?"

Nate extended the document.

"Qu'est-ce que c'est?"

"Um, I . . ."

"Ah . . . what is this?"

"I apologize for disturbing, sir, but that is a message from command."

"Bien."

The general broke the wax seal and spent a minute or two reading the communiqué. His expression changed to deep concern.

"If this is accurate, I have been tricked by Cornwallis, and my men are in for *un assaut de surprise*."

"Anasso dih surpreez?"

"Surprise attack."

"I don't know anything about . . . "

"Come with me."

Lafayette turned his horse and cantered the animal through the trees to the edge of the James River. Nate urged on Milk, and they caught up when Lafayette stopped by the river's edge. He looked long and hard down the shoreline toward the east.

"All reports had Cornwallis moving his main army across the river," the general said. "But, *au contraire*, the report you delivered says our patriot friends on the other side have seen no indication that a large force has landed."

"They're still over on this side?"

"If they are, I have sent my men *en masse* into a trap," Lafayette said and, again, looked intently down the shoreline. "They would be hidden by *la crête* near the shoreline down by that curve in the river." He balled up a fist in frustration. "I must know."

When Congress gave Lafayette his commission as a general, they thought the young man would be a figurehead of sorts and never actually lead men into battle. Fortunately for America, General Washington met

Lafayette, and the two men instantly became friends and stayed so for their lifetimes. Washington was impressed with the Frenchman's intelligence and commitment to liberty and put him on the battlefield. Lafayette demonstrated courage, tactical skill, and great leadership at the battles of Brandywine (where he was wounded), Barren Hill, Monmouth, and Rhode Island. In 1781, Washington gave Lafayette the task of defending Virginia with fewer than six thousand troops. The British army outnumbered them by more than two thousand experienced soldiers and had vastly superior equipment.

"Maybe we could see them from out there," Nate suggested and pointed the other way up the shoreline to a long spit that jutted out into the river. Lafayette looked at the spit and the view it would offer.

"*Bon!* Excellent suggestion."

To get to the tip of the spit, the horses had to slog through deep mud and thick underbrush, but they made it in only a few minutes. Nate and the general dismounted and walked to a brush-covered spot by the waterline.

A mile or so down the James, the riverbank and surrounding woods were quiet, but, at the base of the trees, there was unmistakable movement that looked to Nate like an army of red-coated ants.

"A lot of them," he whispered.

"*Mon Dieu!* Too many," Lafayette replied and led Nate at a quick clip back to their horses.

To the boy's complete amazement, General Lafayette handed the reins of his horse to Nate.

"You must get word to General Wayne *immédiatement*. He is moving directly toward the trap. Tell him to *rétracter . . .*"

"Raytraktay, sir?"

". . . retreat to the northwest end of the causeway where I will direct a fallback line. You understand?"

"Yes, but . . ."

"*Rapidement!* Speed is everything!"

Nate swung up onto the fantastic horse and in seconds was going faster than he thought possible.

General Lafayette reached up, grabbed a handful of Milk's mane, and swung himself up onto the wide back. Sergeant Harrington had been partially right. When the need arose, Milk could sort of gallop. The draft horse and the general lumbered through the woods back toward the staging area and Lafayette's uncommitted troops.

Nate was riding a rocket. The black horse was running so fast that the trees passed by in a blur as they angled away from the riverbank, through an open field, and back the way they had come. Turning on even more speed, the Thoroughbred stretched his long legs, and they burst through a wooded area like they had been shot from a gun.

Just another half a mile and they would reach General Wayne and his troops. Nate was exhilarated by the high-speed ride and the knowledge that he was carrying out an important mission for none other than General Lafayette himself!

Just then, two British soldiers, doing clandestine reconnaissance of the American troop strength, blocked the road, stopped the general's horse, and held a sword point to Nate's throat.

Chapter 7

Thirty-year-old Sergeant Nigel Purdie looked Nate over and said, "Well, what have we here, then?"

The British army had probably saved Purdie from either an early demise or a life behind bars. By age nineteen, Purdie knew the local authorities in his English town were hot on his heels for a series of alleyway robberies. One night, a British army recruiter was in a tavern buying ale for all and spinning glorious stories of adventure and glory in the mighty British army. Purdie had no military aspirations, but he certainly warmed to free ale and the recruiter's offer of ten pounds sterling to any man who would join that night. Money and escape. Purdie signed up on the spot.

"A loyalist!" Nate said with a wide smile and much enthusiasm. "I feared I might well have to ride a great distance to find compatriots!" he fabricated.

"He looks more like a patriot than a compatriot to me," Private Paul Boone said with a sneer.

"Ha!" Nate said in an offended tone. "Call me a weasel or a snake or a buzzard, but do not call me a patriot! I will not be insulted by alignment with the vermin who trampled my family's fields, burned our barns, and ransacked our home!"

"That's a French saddle," Purdie observed.

"And too fine a mount for a boy," added Boone.

"Where did you get that horse?" Purdie demanded.

"Ask that of the French officer who lies still on the ground," Nate said. "If he is able to converse, he might recall the blow struck his head by a boy with the sword of a British dragoon!"

Nate pulled Sergeant Adickes's sword from its scabbard. Boone whipped up his pistol, but Nate held his weapon out flat on his open palms. Purdie took the sword and looked it over.

"'Tis a fine dragoon blade true," he said, "though a victim of flame."

"Flames set to my house by dog-eared patriots!" Nate said passionately.

"Dragoons give up their blade to no man. Certainly not to a boy," Purdie responded with a certain amount of pride and defiance.

"Maybe the blow he claims to have delivered went to the back of the head of an unsuspecting dragoon," Boone said, "and he stole the sword from a dead man like a jackal."

"Perhaps the dragoon who gave his life helping run the patriots from my family's farm would like to know his sword has been referred to as the spoils of a jackal," Nate retorted. "As would, I imagine, the British officer who gave it to me along with this fine linen shirt."

"I'll take the boy back through the woods and on to camp," Purdie said to Boone. "You assume a shielded position and keep keen eye on the roadway."

Boone nodded but knew that, as soon as the overbearing sergeant was out of sight, he would find a safe, shady spot and take a nap. He was not about to risk his life and limb for Purdie, the army, or anyone else.

"Headquarters will sort this out," Purdie continued and motioned for Nate to dismount.

"All because my father proudly flew the British flag and stood firm in his support of His Majesty King George?!" Nate said incredulously. "Pray tell, what matter of loyalty does a British soldier demand? Have your battles destroyed your belief in the rights of an Englishman? For what do you fight then?"

Nate did not realize the effect his words would have, but his question struck a strong chord in Purdie.

Three weeks after Purdie joined the army, he was ready to desert and take his chances with the law, but weeks turned into months and, to his surprise, Purdie began to like being a soldier. Promoted to sergeant after a few years, he became a hard taskmaster, and his men resented his by-the-book methods and humorless discipline. Heaven help a soldier who disparaged the military, the British Empire, or King George. Sergeant Purdie had become, as some of his disgruntled men said, a believer.

"I will ride down this road and retrieve my mother and sister from a hiding place in the woods," Nate said, reading the look on Purdie's face. "If you want to shoot a man in the back for being loyal to the King and for saving a good woman and innocent little girl, go ahead."

Looking the sergeant dead in the eye, Nate leaned down and took his sword from Purdie, who, surprisingly, did not react.

Nate said, "Sort *that* out, sir."

Nate turned the big horse, brushed past Boone, and galloped away. Boone raised his musket and aimed it at Nate's back. Purdie reached over, grabbed the man's wrist, and lowered the weapon. Nate and the horse disappeared around a bend in the road.

"Stay lively and keep alert," Purdie said to Boone.

In your eye, Boone thought, but gave his sergeant a crisp salute. Purdie started making his way back to the British camp, and Boone went searching for a nice spot to take a nap.

As he pushed the black steed to a full run, Nate began trembling and had to wipe away the rivulets of sweat that suddenly came pouring down his face and into his eyes.

Another half a mile and Nate got his first real taste of war. American troops were marching toward rear British positions that they thought were thinly defended. Two cannons were booming their missiles toward the area as the line of American soldiers moved steadily and methodically toward their objective. The Continentals marched with confidence, but the tension in the air was strong. Captains were on horseback, trotting back and forth in front of the infantrymen, shouting orders and encouragement.

A group of three senior officers including General Wayne sat motionless on their horses watching the drama unfold. Only one man stopped Nate, but he recognized General Lafayette's horse and waved the boy over toward the senior officers.

At that moment, a British force of a stunningly large size emerged from the woods. The trap was sprung. The red-coated infantry fired in precisely staggered and deadly volleys. Nate felt his heart in his throat as he watched American soldiers go down; some lay motionless, others writhed in pain, still others tried to pull themselves up and rejoin the battle on injured limbs. The barely contained bedlam of the scene was somehow detached from reality, but the noise, smoke, and screams were very real. The American forces were turning back, and the battle was threatening to become a rout of redcoats running down a scattered and panicked foe.

Nate forced himself back to the job at hand. He galloped over to the officers and yelled over the battle noise:

"General Wayne!"

There was no response as the veteran general stared at the battlefield sorting rapid-fire through the options clicking off in his head.

"General!" Nate shouted again. "A message from General Lafayette!"

A colonel heard Nate and tugged at his commander's arm. General Wayne turned.

"General Lafayette knows of the trap!" Nate said loudly into the general's ear. "He said to fall back to the far end of the causeway where he will be commanding a position!"

General Wayne understood, nodded, and said to the colonel, "They must be regrouped for the fallback, or it will be a slaughter. Mount a two-volley charge, and then retreat to Lafayette's position."

"A charge!?" The colonel asked incredulously.

"Now!"

"Yes, sir!"

The young colonel galloped down the rise toward the battle. He ran his horse up and down through the melee shouting orders. Continental drums rose above the sounds of battle and beat out the signal to charge! The officers echoed the order at the top of their lungs. Their troops stopped, turned, loosely regrouped, and fired a volley at the rapidly advancing redcoats. Then the American infantrymen ran dead at the British and fired another volley. The brash charge temporarily confused the British troops, and they retreated thirty yards.

The fifes and drums cried out for retreat, and the patriots did. Only now it was a more orderly retreat with cover fire and no panic. General Wayne spurred his horse down to the men and led the double-time march back through the woods and across the causeway where they would join Lafayette and his waiting troops. Unsure what to do, Nate rode after the general.

There was still constant musket fire from the British troops as Nate spurred the horse and caught up to the infantrymen. Suddenly, a private let out a yell and fell over to the ground in agony. There was a nasty red hole in his tunic, and the crimson circle was expanding. Nate stopped the horse, jumped down, and kneeled next to the injured man.

"Aaaaaaaargh," the man moaned. "Aaaaaaa, 'tis a bad hit, I fear. Ah! Ah! Ah!"

"I'll get you back," Nate reassured the man.

"Oooooooh, sweet Lord! Aaaaaaaargh!"

"Sit up! Help me!"

Nate yanked the man up to a sitting position, kneeled next to him, and draped the wounded soldier's arm over his shoulder.

"We're standing now! Up!"

The soldier let out a scream of pain as he and Nate rose to a standing position and shuffled over to Lafayette's horse. Somehow, Nate got the man's foot into the stirrup and pushed him up into the saddle. The boy swung up behind the wounded man, and they galloped toward the causeway. Musket balls were whistling through the air and shredding foliage on either side of the trail.

At the far end of the causeway, two soldiers lifted the wounded man from Nate's mount and put him on a stretcher. Just before the man lapsed into unconsciousness, he gave Nate a look of profound thanks. Several captured British soldiers were under guard. One of them was Private Boone, and the look he gave Nate was less kind. Before the boy could react, General Lafayette rode up on Milk.

"How do you do, sir," Nate said.

"I have received reports on your mission," the general said sternly.

Nate looked nervous and intimidated.

"And *un prisonnier de guerre* spins quite a tale about how you talked your way past his swords and pistols."

"Well, sir, I . . ."

"Excellent work, young sir! You are quite *ingénieux!* I have other demands at present, but I ask that you report to me in Williamsburg in two days."

"Yes, sir!" Nate beamed.

"Au revoir!" Lafayette said and trotted off a few feet before stopping. "One more item."

"Yes, sir?"

"I wonder if you might be interested in swapping that old mount for this fine steed that has carried me so admirably and without protest?"

"I . . . of course, general."

Embarrassed, Nate jumped to the ground.

Laughing, the general sprang up on his horse's back.

"Au revoir!" he called and rode away to his troops.

Nate climbed up onto Milk's back and took a look around. He could see that Lafayette's decision to marshal his troops at the end of the causeway was smart. The swamp passage was so narrow that superior British numbers were meaningless as only so many men at a time could march across the causeway. Lafayette's plan had been a good one. In reality, however, it was the fact that darkness was rapidly approaching that led the British commander, Lord Cornwallis, to forego further conflict. By morning, his troops had crossed the James River and were long gone. Lafayette and the patriots considered the battle a victory.

Within two hours, the wounded had been attended and other mop-up duties performed. The American soldiers returned to camp to sit around their fires eating and rehashing the day's heroics. By then, the story of Nate bamboozling the British soldiers had been thoroughly churned through the rumor mill, and several versions floated through the camp. One variation even had the boy claiming to be King George's nephew. No matter, the tale cemented Nate as a brave lad, and he was welcomed by the soldiers. He enjoyed the camaraderie and spent a pleasant evening eating and laughing with the men. An aide to General Lafayette brought over a bucket of fine oats for Milk, and a good night's sleep was had by all.

In the morning, Nate felt better than he had since the gruesome raid on the farm. He was beginning to feel like a part of something and could partially see past his personal vendetta to the bigger picture of revolution. But, before he returned to Williamsburg, he intended to go out on his own to check the now-empty British positions for any sign of Rex and then go see his parents.

General Lafayette and his top aides left late in the night for Williamsburg. The Frenchman knew General Washington needed some good news as it was not going well for the commander of the Continental army up north. Washington was nearly obsessed with retaking New York from the British, who had occupied the city since September 1776. As serious a problem as the British fortifications around the city and their powerful fleet in the harbor was the condition of the Continental troops. The Continental Congress was nearly bankrupt, and the unhappy soldiers had not been paid in months. Their uniforms were raggedy and food rations slim. Lafayette would see to it that reports, only slightly embellished, of the battle were dispatched to Washington in New York immediately.

The next morning, after taking care of that and similar tasks, General Lafayette called in James. The slave stood respectfully in front of Lafayette's desk.

"I understand that you have *une telle mémoire,*" the general said.

"Well, sir, I suppose it like a man who can paint a good portrait or play a fine fiddle. It don't seem like much to him, but others seem to think it a gift of sorts."

Lafayette looked at James for a few seconds.

"When you passed through *le quartier général,* what did you see?"

"Beggin' the general's pardon, but, if I passed through leh karteeay jaynayral, I wa'n't aware of it."

Lafayette smiled and said, "Headquarters."

"Oh. Everything I seed?"

"Everything."

"Hmm, well, sir, when you walk inside, there's a little raised place on the sill with a good iron nail stickin' out that could go right on through a foot if a man a'n't careful. Over on the one side there, a left-handed man with two stripes on his sleeves and red hair and a cut ear was writin' on a three-page paper of some kind or other. Above his head, there was a hangin' a paintin' of a young girl holdin' a pet squirrel with a red ribbon 'round his neck. The little girl has a pink satin sash 'round her waist which is tied in a real nice bow over on her right side. She's a wearin' little yella shoes, and I believe I recall a gold chain 'round her right wrist that has some kind'a red stone on it. Now, I'm sure the frame on the paintin' is a fine thing, but there is a big chip out of it down there towards the bottom left corner."

James closed his eyes for a second and continued.

"Now, if I look on over to the other side, I see . . ."

General Lafayette held up his hand for James to stop.

"*Une minute,*" he said and left the office.

He walked across the hall to where a red-headed, left-handed corporal was writing beneath a portrait of Hannah and her pet squirrel. Every detail was exactly as James had recounted. Smiling, Lafayette went back into his office.

After learning of his training as a house slave, the best use of James's talents was clear to General Lafayette. Within only a few hours, the plan was worked out and under way.

Reports had Lord Cornwallis moving his entire army to Yorktown. James was hidden in the back of a wagon and dropped four miles outside of that York River town. The slave stayed out of sight until he spotted a contingent of British dragoons. Colonel Banastre Tarleton was leading the legion. Sergeant Clinton Adickes rode to his right. James took a deep breath and stepped out into the road in front of the heavily armed cavalrymen.

"Thank the Lord!" James exclaimed.

"Out of my way," Tarleton said.

"Oh, yes indeed, sir. I'll get out yo way. I was jest hoping you could point me towards some fine British officer who could use the services of a man trained in all the finest points of caterin' to a gentleman's needs."

"What are you doing out here?" Tarleton demanded.

"I heard 'bout the royal gov'ner sayin' that, if a slave join up with the English soldiers, he be a free man. Now, I can't shoot no musket or swing no sword, but I set as fine a table as you ever seen, and I can lay out a gentleman's clothes and serve a glass of fine wine good as anybody, better'n most."

"Shall I cut off his head?" Adickes asked.

"Oh, Jesus!" James whimpered.

"No," Colonel Tarleton said. "Command is displeased with their immediate servants so I hear. Perhaps this dimwit can be of service."

"Oh, thank you, sir!" James gushed.

"We'll keep him with us until Lord Cornwallis's forward force reaches Yorktown on the morrow. Put him on a horse."

"Goshamighty! I a'n't much on no horse!" James wailed.

"Or cut off his head."

"I can do fine on a horse, sir! Jest fine on a horse!"

James really was not much of a horseman, but he managed to hang on for the rest of the afternoon as he tagged along behind the dragoons. Thankfully, there was no combat, and the cavalrymen seemed to be doing nothing more than sweeping the general area around Yorktown before the main army's arrival.

By dusk, the dragoons were in their makeshift camp near the York, dismounted and settling their horses and themselves in for the night. In another hour, the soldiers were eating beef cooked over an open fire. Colonel Tarleton's tent was closed, and only the occasional aide was allowed to enter.

After the dragoons were full, the lowest-ranking private was dispatched to take a metal plate of burned fat and bones to James, who was sitting under a tree at the edge of the camp. The private walked up to the slave and, from waist high, dropped the plate on the ground and walked away laughing. The food was dusty but edible. As he chewed on a piece of fat, James watched an obviously drunk Sergeant Adickes stagger away from the fire. The ratty little man carried a torch and drank from a bottle as he weaved down into a small stand of trees. James gave Adickes no more thought until he heard a weak but somehow familiar bark come from the dark.

A chain was attached to Rex's leather collar and then locked around a tree trunk. The big dog had lost a lot of weight in only a few days, but, worse, there were ominous burn marks, cuts, and matted, bloody places all over his body and head. His left front paw was swollen to twice its normal size. Rex looked terrible, but his blue eyes did not look beaten and they flashed when he got Adickes's scent. When the sergeant came into view, Rex pulled himself up, strained at the chain, and barked as loudly as he could.

"Defy me still, do you?" Adickes slurred and glared at Rex with bleary red eyes. "There be a day soon when you'll whimper at my feet! No dumb animal alive don't cower to Clinton Adickes! When that day comes, then I kill you!"

He raised the torch and crashed it down again and again.

James waited until he was sure Sergeant Adickes was passed out in his tent before he made his way down to the trees. Although Rex was lying on his side gasping for breath, he still managed to wag his tail when he smelled James approaching. He wagged it even more when the slave gave him the fat and the bones.

It took James a few minutes to saw through Rex's collar with a sharp-edged rock. They found a small spring, and Rex drank for minutes.

"You mus' git on out'a here now, Rex. You won't live another day 'round here. Git on!" James whispered.

Rex took a few steps but then came back to James.

"No, boy. Git yoself goin'."

Rex leaned against James and stayed put.

James thought a few seconds and then said, "You git them cows home, Rex. Nate needs you to git them cows."

That did it. Rex began walking off into the night. He stopped once and looked back at James, who pointed west and said again, "Git them cows home, boy. Find Nate."

Rex limped through the woods for a while and then followed the edge of the road. It was very dark, and Rex had nothing but a stomach full of beef fat and instinct to get him home.

Chapter 8

Rex walked all night and most of the next morning. His foot hurt so badly that he eventually held it up and shuffled along on three legs. Slowly, painfully, he pushed on to the Chandler farm or what was left of it. As Rex moved down the familiar trail toward the farm, his ears were up in anticipation of seeing Nate and his cows, but the only life among the burned-out ruins was a group of buzzards feeding on the wild pig carcass.

Rex managed a weak bark and a half-hearted charge, enough to send the big birds up into a tree. They did not go far, however, as Rex looked to be a promising meal soon. The vultures had stripped the pig of all meat, but there were plenty of bones for Rex to gnaw. He lay down and chewed a thick hip bone until it was gone. The nutritional marrow pushed some energy through his battered body, and Rex made his way down to the creek.

The big dog eased down into the slow-moving flow. He swam over to a half-submerged stump and leaned against it. He rested his head on the stump and closed his eyes. For more than an hour, the water flowed around Rex, washing his wounds and easing the swelling in his foot. By the time he left the stream and stretched out in the shade, the dog was a bit better, and the buzzards gave up and flew away. Rex slept soundly for six straight hours.

When Rex woke up, he felt stronger. Much of the pain was gone, and his foot was approaching normal size. He ate another pig bone and then started following his master's scent back down the trail.

*****

At dawn on the same morning, American sergeants mustered their troops for the march to Williamsburg. They left in high spirits knowing they had met the enemy and held their own. Nate did not leave with the soldiers. He rode Milk to the abandoned British encampment to look for his dog.

The British camp close to the James River shoreline was barren except for campfire remains, some trash, and the trampled earth left by horses, men, wagons, and cannons. There were some stray dogs competing with the foxes and raccoons for whatever they could find, but Rex was not among them. Nate called out his dog's name loudly and often, but there was no response.

Nate dismounted, tied Milk to a tree, and walked around. He was not looking for anything in particular, just some sign that Rex was alive. As he moved down next to the sandy river shoreline, he thought he saw movement behind a dead tree that had fallen halfway over into the water.

"Rex!" he shouted hopefully. "Rex!"

But there was no response. He cautiously made his way over to the tree.

"Screeeeeee!"

A bizarre creature with long trails of filthy matted hair, inch-long claws, and bony yellow skin jumped out at him!

"Yah!" Nate yelped in surprise.

He jumped back a few feet and drew his sword, but there was no need for the weapon. The old lady held up a little hatchet, but her spindly arms were like pieces of veined thread, and her eyes were too soft to be dangerous.

"This camp is mine," she croaked and then coughed loudly. "You go and scavenge somewhere else."

War introduced some interesting career choices. Soldiering, of course, not to mention the endless array of goods and services it took to keep an army running kept many people busy and employed. Tradesmen had to make the uniforms, muskets, saddles, blankets, and wagons. Farmers grew food for the troops. Vendors sold their wares to privates and generals alike. Horses were bought and sold, clothes were washed, meals were cooked, and on and on.

A somewhat-lower rung on the food chain was occupied by scavengers, people who lived by their wits because they had no skills or money to otherwise keep themselves whole. They were the hyenas of war, creeping around the camps looking for scraps of almost anything. What an army regarded as refuse, a scavenger saw as opportunity. They ate food scraps and dressed in discarded uniforms, flags, and rags. They built fires from broken wagon wheels. They gathered up every piece of metal and bartered it for basic needs. Nate noticed the large canvas bag that hung from her shoulder. Part of a British flagpole protruded along with several pieces of slightly burned firewood. The outline of a horseshoe was toward the bottom of the bag.

"No, no, madam," Nate said. "I'm here but to look for my dog. Anything else, I say, belongs to you without contest."

He sheathed his sword. The old lady narrowed her eyes and looked Nate over.

"How 'bout them lead musket balls in the trees and ground? I can dig'm out and trade'm wit a man for peaches."

"And the peaches you should have. I'm just looking for my dog."

"Hrumph, there's a couple of mangy critters up above there might pass for dogs."

"I saw them. Not my dog. How long have you been around here?"

"Ever since them sorry redcoats come a marchin' in. They're a sad bunch. Won't give a lady a beg your pardon. Now, ten years ago, they'd a been flutterin' 'round me like hummin' birds on a red lily."

"I've no doubt of it," Nate said. "Did you see a big gold dog? Really big. Floppy ears, blue eyes?"

"No. I a'n't seen no dogs 'cept them ratty mongrels up the rise."

Nate exhaled.

"I see. Thank you for your time."

He gave the old lady a courteous bow and turned to leave.

"Don't git to thinkin' 'bout them musket balls when you pass over that battlefield."

"No, no. I'll be riding straight on past that."

"Hope you find your dog," the old lady said and then started a violent coughing fit.

Nate gave her a nod, walked to Milk, and started out. He never considered the possibility that he would not find his dog. That was an additional sadness he would not allow to happen. It just couldn't.

When Nate arrived at Miss Albright's house later that day, he learned that his father had been battling a fever that had broken only that morning. Between the fever and his severe wounds, William's body was wrung out, and he was in a deep state of sleep.

"'Tis no better treatment for him," Dr. Averett said. "Sleep is the good Lord's most potent medicine."

Rachel could still barely move, but she sat next to her husband and kept a cool rag on his head. Nate dipped the cloth in a basin of water and handed it to his mother.

"What of his leg?" he asked Dr. Averett.

"Out of our hands," Dr. Averett answered. "All has been done that can be done."

After the doctor left, Nate debated whether or not to tell his mother about the total destruction of the farm. He decided it best to be truthful about it. She listened but, to Nate's surprise, did not seem upset by the news.

With her good hand, she indicated Nate, William, and herself and whispered, "All that's important."

Rachel sat stone still as Nate told her he had joined the army and why. His mother looked off into space for a full silent minute, and Nate was sure she was going to plead with him to reconsider and stay with her and William.

She turned her eyes to him. After a few shallow breaths, she said in a hoarse whisper, "I understand."

Nate and Milk got to Williamsburg by early evening. It was like riding into a carnival. The lingering joy of the British troops leaving town had been amplified by the, as the stories had it, glorious American victory. Although their number was not great, everyone left in town was out on the streets. Greetings were warm, and the general atmosphere was one of great cheer. Several infantrymen were cheered as they made their way down Duke of Gloucester Street guiding a cannon pulled by a team of horses. The tavern front doors were wide open, and each appeared to be full of happy and boisterous patrons. Even though they had few wares to sell, shop owners welcomed customers with effusive greetings.

Although the battle had been a draw at best, the town embraced one irrefutable fact: there had been fighting followed by the British troops abandoning the battlefield and crossing the James. American heroes had sent the redcoats fleeing in mortal fear was the general idea, and it was a morale boost the forces needed.

It was hard not to get caught up in the excitement, and Nate was not immune despite the nagging concern over Rex. Since his appointment with General Lafayette was not until the next day, Nate decided to investigate the scene. The streets were clogged with all manner of wagons, carts, coaches, horses, and oxen. Nate rode almost to the end of Duke of Gloucester Street, down near the old Capitol, before he found a spot where he could tie Milk to a post. He straightened up his shirt, brushed away the road dust, and took a stroll.

Two years earlier, the capital of the most successful of the British colonies, Virginia, had been moved from Williamsburg to Richmond because its inland location was perceived to be safer. During its eighty-plus-year reign as capital, Williamsburg had been a lively, exciting, even glamorous city. Perhaps it was because of the embargos, encamped troops, or change in political status, but, to Nate, now the residents seemed not quite as well dressed, the shops not quite as shiny, and the streets dirtier.

"Lo and behold!" Isaac, a large man in a Continental uniform, bellowed as he exited the Raleigh Tavern with a group of other merry soldiers. "Yet another hero of the glorious battle stands before us!"

Nate recognized Isaac as one of the men who had been sitting around the campfire eating after the engagement with the British.

"Well, Isaac," he laughed, "you seem to be of good cheer."

"Indeed, my boy! Indeed! I trust you will honor us with your company for rations this evening."

"Thank you. Where are you camped?"

Isaac pointed down the street.

"Over near the courthouse."

"You're not at the plantation?"

"No, no, we're all encamped in or near Williamsburg now. Late for muster. Farewell to you!"

Isaac and the others weaved away. Nate smiled as he watched the men gallantly swoop their hats and flirt with every woman they passed on the street. He was feeling better. Tonight, he and Milk would have good rations and a place to sleep. Tomorrow, he would meet with General Lafayette and see what the war held in store for him. Whatever it was, Nate hoped it would somehow lead him to his dog.

Nate enjoyed watching the market activity and general comings and goings in Williamsburg until the sun began to set. He rode Milk to the palace green where many of the military horses were fenced. Sergeant Harrington was glad to see the big draft horse and put him in a small corral for the night. Nate was hungry and made his way over to the group of tents set up on the grounds around the courthouse. After a few minutes, he found Isaac and his cohorts gathered around a fire cooking chicken over the open flame.

The boy was welcomed, and, within an hour, Nate and the men were full, but there was more to come. Two thoughtful local ladies walked among the tents handing out freshly baked sweets to the soldiers. Isaac, Nate, and the others at their fire watched the ladies move closer and closer to their position. To a man, they were afraid the baskets would be empty by the time the good Samaritans reached them, but their luck held. Each of them got a sugar-covered molasses cake that was, as Isaac said, a little chip of heaven.

Happy and full, it was time for the soldiers to spin tales about the battle. Nate was puzzled that he did not remember most of the heroics the men described, but he had not seen everything. Then the attention focused on him, just as Sergeant Harrington walked up and joined the group.

"This boy," Isaac said, "fought his way through a solid wall of redcoat sabers and muskets to deliver a message from General Lafayette himself. He slashed his way up the hill and made it to General Wayne just in the nick of time."

"That's not exactly what . . ."

"Then he charged back down the hill fighting side by side with the general, only stopping to pick up a wounded man on the battlefield. He threw the man over his shoulder and carried him two miles to safety."

"No, no, . . . I was actually on a horse and . . ."

"Huzzah for this boy! I say, huzzah!"

The other men shouted out "Huzzah!" and held up their cups to Nate.

Nate stood up and said, "Listen! I didn't do . . ."

"A moment, sir," Sergeant Harrington said to Nate. "There is something we must discuss."

He stood and motioned sternly for Nate to follow.

"Now."

After they got a few yards from the other men, Sergeant Harrington asked, "What were you about to say back there?"

"That what Isaac was saying about me was not true."

"It would be a mistake to talk that way."

"But that wasn't what happened."

"Maybe they know that a little, but there is more to it. The most important thing in a battle is not how many muskets, swords, or cannons you have. It is that you believe you can defeat the enemy. Heroes and grand feats of courage support that belief, inspire men to believe they can win. An army without heroics will not win battles or the hearts of their countrymen."

"Even if the heroes are made up?"

"Especially then, my boy."

They walked across the green and angled toward a big house set on the corner.

"General Lafayette is ready to see you now," Harrington said.

"Now? Tonight?"

"Inside," the sergeant said. "Good luck."

Sergeant Harrington walked away. Nate looked up at the house, which served as temporary headquarters for the marquis de Lafayette. To Nate, it seemed a grand structure and intimidating. It was not a lavish palace by any means but was large, handsome, roomy, and the height of comfort for a family of lofty stature in the community.

The house was dimly lit and busy. Officers, enlisted men, and local noncombatants were in, out, and all around the house. It was not easy, but Nate finally made it up to the front door and told a servant his name. The man went inside, returned in a few minutes, and ushered the boy through another group of officers in the entry hall and down a hallway to the room converted into an office.

Lafayette was studying maps by candlelight but looked up when the servant said, "Mr. Nate Chandler, sir." The general nodded and went back to his maps. The servant indicated that Nate should go in. He took a few steps into the room and stood in front of the Frenchman's desk. Several minutes passed with no acknowledgment from Lafayette. To Nate, it seemed like an uncomfortable lifetime.

At last, the general looked up and said, "What were you thinking when you told the bounty hunter the Thomas Jefferson tale?"

"Thinking, sir?"

"Yes, was there deep thought?"

"Oh, . . . no, no. It just . . . happened."

"I see. And when the British soldiers stopped you on the road? Did you have the ruse about your family being loyalists thought out prior to the incident?"

Nate was nervous. The general did not look pleased and probably thought him a dunce, but he told the truth.

"No. Again, sir, it just seemed to come out of my mouth. I have no explanation for my actions."

"Aha. One last question. When you helped the wounded man, *avais-tu-peur?*"

"Sir?"

"Were you afraid?"

Nate exhaled and thought for a second.

"Afraid before and after, general, but not during."

"Hmm."

General Lafayette stood and walked over to a window. He clasped his hands behind his back and looked out at the night for what seemed like an eternity. Nate was sure he had said all the wrong things and would soon be assigned stable boy duties at best.

Lafayette finally turned and said, "Spies often have no time to plan, only react. *De bons agents secrets* have an inherent ability to adapt quickly to any situation. Great spies do so instinctively." The general smiled. "I believe you will be a great one."

"A great . . . spy?"

"I'll be counting on you a great deal." Lafayette extended his hand and Nate clasped it. "Captain Rawlinson will discuss the plan with you in some detail. Now, I must get back to more mundane matters."

"Thank you, general, sir," was all Nate could get out.

"*Au revoir.*"

The plan was relatively simple and left a lot of room for Nate to improvise when necessary. On a deserted and overgrown farm about a mile and a half southwest of Yorktown, Nate would find a storage bin full of dried corn. Every day, Nate was to fill up a basket with corn and wander the British encampment trying to sell the produce to soldiers who would grind it into cornmeal to supplement their rations. His real mission was to take note of numbers of troops, armament, movement, and anything else of interest Cornwallis's army was doing.

"Lord Cornwallis and his troops are filtering into Yorktown now," Captain Rawlinson said. "Within a few days, we hope to have the other side of the equation in place."

"What would that be, sir?'

"A man inside Cornwallis's command headquarters. We do not know, however, if our man will be able to actually breach that inner circle."

"Who is the man?"

"James, the slave."

"He'll breach it, sir."

"God willing."

"Where is James now?"

"We don't know."

By midnight, Sergeant Harrington had provided Nate with everything he needed, including a worn farmer's shirt to replace the one he had removed from the dragoon. Despite his reluctance, Nate also exchanged his sword for a hunting knife, relying on Sergeant Harringon's promise to keep the dragoon saber safe. Milk was at his disposal.

Nate tried to sleep but was so excited by the prospects of the next day that he tossed and turned on a straw pad near the horse pens until he finally gave up at four thirty and put a bridle on Milk. By five, they were a mile outside of Williamsburg on the road to Yorktown.

At seven thirty, Nate saw the man who had injured his parents and destroyed his home. Coming toward him, Sergeant Adickes led a squad of seven dragoons and a slave along the road. The group trotted directly toward Nate and Milk. Nate's vision blurred with rage. He felt a compulsion to rip at Adickes's face and eyes with his bare hands, but he fought off the immediate lust for revenge. Soon, he thought, soon, you animal, but not now.

The boy guided the draft horse over to the side of the road so the soldiers could pass. He pulled his hat low over his face and looked down. If Adickes should recognize him, the great spy mission would be over before it began.

As the group passed him without comment, James and Nate held a millisecond look, but nothing else. The last of the dragoons rode by, and Nate exhaled with relief at not being seen and for not jumping on Adickes and stabbing him with the hunting knife. Just as Nate was going to continue his ride to Yorktown, Sergeant Adickes suddenly pulled up his horse and looked back over his shoulder. For the briefest of instants, his eyes met those of the farm boy on the draft horse.

The dragoon sergeant's face went scary. As he turned his horse and dug his spurs into the animal's sides, he pulled his pistol from his belt. With the gun leveled straight out, he charged back through his men and dead for Nate and Milk.

Chapter 9

Nate knew he was about to die, but he intended to take Sergeant Adickes with him. Although only a second or two had passed since the man began his charge, it seemed like slow motion to the boy, and his brain was searching for the right signal to transmit to his eyes and hands. Another half a second passed; Adickes was ten yards away at a full gallop. Nate's hand went to the handle of his hunting knife. Another second and it was now or never. The knife came out of his belt when the horse was so close Nate could feel the animal's breath. Lunge! His brain was commanding. Lunge and stab before a pistol ball strikes your heart!

But the cavalry horse left the ground, flying! Over the fence by Nate and Milk! Twenty yards across the field and BAM! A large cow staggered, fell to its knees, then slumped down dead from the shot to his head.

Laughing, Adickes reared up his horse and yelled, "More beef for my boys!"

He jumped the horse back over the fence and spurred him past Nate without a glance. The dragoons all galloped away toward Yorktown. Bringing up the rear, James managed a quick look back to Nate. His mind was racing trying to figure out a signal that would tell Nate that Rex was alive and free, but there was no opportunity.

Nate's heart was beating so loudly in his ears that he could not think. The knife dropped to the ground, and he sat like a statue for a few minutes. Then, he dismounted, picked up the knife, and began walking. Milk followed. After a mile, the boy's breathing was normal and his head cleared. He climbed back up on the draft horse and continued his mission.

*****

The dragoons and James rode into Yorktown, and it was a busy place indeed. Approximately eight thousand British and German troops were setting up their tents, positioning cannons, quartering supplies, and constructing redoubts. These raised forts along the trenches were constructed of packed earth; to slow attackers, they were fortified with sharpened stakes midway up the walls and with tangles of tree trunks, limbs, and other debris along their bases.

Along with hired diggers and some British infantrymen, hundreds of defected slaves were digging an elaborate series of trenches. James had heard that many of the runaway slaves had been put into Lord Cornwallis's Ethiopian Guard and wore fancy uniforms, but there were no fancy uniforms here. Diggin' them trenches look ever bit as hard as pickin' tobacco, he thought to himself. And I imagine the pay 'bout the same.

British ships were docked and unloading various munitions and provisions. Lord Cornwallis and his staff were setting up their headquarters at the commandeered home of Thomas Nelson, former colony secretary and uncle to the governor of Virginia. The activity was orderly and executed with the disciplined efficiency of a well-trained and long-standing army. James had never seen anything like it and thought to himself that the patriot troops were facing a tough road ahead. He intended to make it easier for them.

Sergeant Adickes and his men were eager to get rid of James and return to their raids in the countryside. They rode up to the Nelson house and dismounted.

Adickes approached a young lieutenant, indicated James, and said, "Colonel Tarleton presents this house slave for consideration."

"I have a battle to prepare for," the lieutenant snipped. "House slaves are not my concern."

"Fine, sir. I'll just then report to Colonel Tarleton that, although he spared eight men to deliver this man to fulfill a need passed to him by senior officers, you, sir, could not be bothered."

The lieutenant glared at the sergeant and finally said, "Leave the man. I'll have it tended to."

"Thank you, sir," Adickes said and gave the young officer a disrespectful salute before he mounted his horse and galloped away.

"Stay here," the officer commanded James, "until you're told to do otherwise."

"I'll stay right here, sir. Ole James a'n't goin' nowhere else at all."

The lieutenant shook his head and stomped into the big house. James sat down on a low wall by the street and waited. He had never actually been to Yorktown and, based on his ride into town and what he was seeing now, concentrated on getting a picture of the terrain and layout in his head. He was giving that some thought when a young kitchen slave exited the house and ran up. The boy was about nine and wore clean houseboy clothes and buckled shoes. His round eyes were forever wide in what looked like a fixed state of surprise.

"Major Castellow want to see you now," the boy said.

"Who is that, pray tell?" James asked.

"He 'bout the meanest man you ever see," the boy replied. "And Lord knows, he don't like waitin' 'round on nobody. Hurry on in there."

Major Hiram Cuthbertson Parke Castellow was unquestionably one of the worst military officers in the entire British army. Like many of his peers, he had purchased his commission with family money, and there was a great deal of that. His own father had given the obnoxious twenty-two year old an ultimatum. Join the military or spend the rest of your life sweltering running a West Indies cane plantation. Hiram had no aptitude for military strategy, no leadership qualities, and zero courage, but the army sounded better than a hot, middle-of-nowhere cane plantation.

Aware of the young major's powerful family position, Lord Cornwallis assigned Castellow two minor military missions early in his career. Both were disasters. In the first, he froze with fear and could not issue any commands at all. In the second, he feigned illness and abandoned his men before a shot was fired.

Unwilling to risk the ire of the Castellow family by sending the man to the gallows or, worse, home, Lord Cornwallis found the perfect job for Castellow. Regally dressed in his custom-tailored uniforms and spit-shined boots of the finest Moroccan leather and his chest full of bogus medals, Major Hiram Castellow was assigned the duty of making sure His Lordship and the generals dined properly. He was very good at it.

One look and James knew the major was a pompous, arrogant nitwit who took himself very seriously. In a way, it was a shame that he was unable to transfer the organizational skills he brought to a kitchen and dining room to the battlefield. No war-hardened field general was ever better prepared for battle than Major Castellow was for dinner. Certainly, no lowly private was ever browbeaten more than the major's kitchen and wait staff.

James's owner, Mr. Armistead, had a blowhard brother much like Castellow, so the slave knew the game. It was simple, really: men like that wanted to be treated like God. When he entered the room where the major sat in a raised velvet chair, James bowed and deferred like he had an audience with King George himself.

"What skills do you claim?" Castellow sniffed.

"Table mostly, sir."

"Slapping some sort of yam concoction onto the wooden plate of a backwoods bumpkin has no connection to cuisine service for His Lordship and his general staff."

"Lord, sir, I can't even imagine such a grand thing. All's I know is sittin' the places and servin' up in a way my master showed me."

"Hrumph, I can just imagine what sterling instruction that must have been."

"He was a rich man."

"Ha! Fortunes made in this heathen wilderness in no way infuse one with grace, style, or appropriate behavior. Bundles of tobacco or whatever it is you people grow over here is no substitute for lineage."

"No, sir, I can see that, sir."

"Eight."

"Excuse me, major, sir."

"Set that table for eight."

James looked over at a long mahogany dining table. A silver service was sitting on a sideboard. It was a familiar setup.

"Immediately."

James took three steps into the adjoining room and opened a drawer in a linen press. As he knew it would, the space contained tablecloths. James stepped back into the dining room, shook out the under cloth, and, with one motion, draped it perfectly over the gleaming table. He repeated the action with a finely embroidered tablecloth. Without any wasted motion, he set fine glassware correctly in front of each place at the table. He followed suit with the silverware, china, and linen napkins. Each piece was as expertly and properly placed as if it had been arranged by His Majesty's own butler. James backed up against the wall and stood demurely with his hands behind his back.

"I know that probly a'n't right at all, major, sir, but that's the way I was taught."

There was a surprised tic in Castellow's right eyelid, but he disguised his wonder at the speed and correctness of the table.

"Madeira," he said.

James went to a wine case and selected a bottle of Madeira wine. He opened it perfectly and then poured into the appropriate glass at each place. He did not spill a drop.

Major Castellow slowly walked around the table. Even though it was perfect, he moved a glass and a fork a fraction of an inch. He stood at the head of the table and cut his eyes back and forth between James and the gleaming settings.

"Henry!" he shouted.

In a second, a tall slave in his sixties wearing a velvet coat and shimmering white shirt and breeches entered.

"Yes, Major Castellow, sir," he said.

"Get this man into a presentable state," the major said. "Starting now, he'll be second assist serve."

James smiled to himself. His mission was to get as close to the British officers, and possibly Lord Cornwallis himself, as possible, and it was beginning to look as if he would be close indeed. At least during mealtimes.

"Yes, sir," the tall man said.

He took James's arm and walked him quickly from the room. The major fidgeted with a napkin for a few seconds and then poured the three inches of wine left in the bottle into a glass and drank it down in one gulp.

*****

As Nate approached Yorktown, he found the turnoff to the deserted farm that would serve as his camp. The narrow trail got smaller and smaller and eventually disappeared completely into a tangle of thick underbrush. Sergeant Harrington had told him to look for a pair of tall, thick holly trees near a rotting old barrel. It took some searching, but Nate finally found the landmark. He dismounted and led Milk around the prickly hollies and through an umbrella of low-hanging evergreens. A few more yards and the abandoned farmhouse came into view. Evidently, it had been years since anyone had occupied the small dwelling, and it was not much more than a grey shell. The roof seemed intact, however, and the shack would provide some shelter.

A storage bin was full of dried corn for Nate to sell to the British. There was a grassy area where Milk could graze. It took the boy a while to clear out a sleeping spot in the house, and then he ate the dried pork and hard biscuits supplied by Sergeant Harrington.

*****

Lord Cornwallis and his general staff were not eating dried pork and hard biscuits. James, Henry, and the young slave boy served His Lordship and the generals oysters, ham, and beef along with a variety of vegetables and breads. James had been instructed to pour the wine and nothing else, and he poured flawlessly. Dressed in his new purple coat and white breeches, he stood silently by the wall between courses and listened.

The conversation centered on Cornwallis's confidence that he would soon get five thousand promised troops from New York and that the British navy would control the area waterways and, therefore, all supply, deployment, and evacuation routes. Word had been received that British Admiral Graves was en route from New York with nineteen ships. Their mission, at least in part, was to run off a fleet of French ships on their way from the West Indies. All of this struck James as information that needed to be passed on to General Lafayette.

After a leisurely meal, Cornwallis and his staff left the table and went about their business. James and the slave boy cleared the table. Even though the meal had gone perfectly, Major Castellow lined up the servers in the dining room and browbeat them about their incompetence. James knew the man would never be happy no matter what they did, so he just ignored the ravings and looked humble, subservient, and intimidated.

While Castellow blustered, James was sorting out the information he had heard at the table in his mind. The plan was for him to pass on intelligence to a free black with American sympathies named George, who was the baker in the headquarters. George would, in turn, give the information to his sister, who would get it to Williamsburg and Lafayette. The problem was that, so far, James had not seen or met George. When the major finally ran out of insults and left the room, James inquired about the baker.

"He been foraging for eggs and good flour, but he oughta be back out in the kitchen by now," Henry said.

James exited the main house and was walking toward the kitchen outbuilding when . . .

"EEEEEEYAHEEEE! Lord! Lord! EEEEEEE!"

James rushed into the kitchen and saw a man flailing around with his shirt on fire! A big cook, Miriam, was chasing after the flaming man, who stumbled and fell screaming to the dirt floor! Reacting, Miriam doused the man with a giant pot of steaming soup, which put out the flames but increased the screaming. James rolled a water barrel across the room and dumped it over the victim. The man stopped screaming but continued to groan and breathe heavily. He was obviously badly burned from both the flames and the soup.

Henry ran in and yelled at Miriam and James, "Gimme that man and clean up this mess! The major'll have a fit he see this!"

Henry tugged the dazed and badly injured man from the kitchen. Miriam and James began cleaning up.

"I told that man and told that man: roll up them sleeves fo you reach in them ovens," Miriam fussed.

She was a very impressive woman who towered over six feet. She held herself with the upright bearing she had inherited from her grandfather, who had been a king in Africa. Miriam's forearms looked like those of a blacksmith, but her eyes had a kind light, and her face often softened with a wide smile.

"Who was that?" James asked.

"He a baker boy who won't be workin' 'round here or nowhere else for a while."

"What's his name?"

"George."

So much for the first link in the intelligence delivery chain. James had not expected to have good information so soon, and now he was at a loss as to how he would get it to Williamsburg.

*****

There were still a couple of hours of daylight left, and Nate was anxious to see Yorktown and the lay of the camp where he was to gather intelligence. He coaxed Milk away from the sweet grass, and they made their way back out to the Yorktown road. Just in case, he filled the deep basket with corn and took it along. He rode toward the town but stopped on a hill near the water. The slaves, diggers, and soldiers were feverishly shoveling out the serpentine trench that would guard the road from Williamsburg. Nate was surprised at the amount of traffic allowed to continue unchecked on to Yorktown. All manner of delivery wagons and carts, raggedy camp followers, tradesmen, produce and fish mongers, and others were streaming down the road toward the British encampment. No one paid the least bit of attention to a farm boy on a draft horse.

Like James, Nate was amazed at the size of the British army camp. At first, he was apprehensive about getting too close to the soldiers, but there were so many other nonmilitary people coming and going that he plucked up his courage and walked into a tent camp.

*****

Miriam told James that she thought George's sister was a laundry woman working the British camp and her name might be Suzy.

"Where the major be 'bout now?" James asked Miriam.

Miriam looked around to make sure no one was watching and then held an imaginary glass up to her lips and drank deeply.

"Hmm," James said, "a imbibin' man."

"He be meaner'n ever here in 'bout two hours," Miriam said.

"I'll be back by then," James said and quickly walked toward the kitchen exit.

"You can't run off like that!" Miriam shouted after him, but James was gone.

Since James was dressed in his fancy purple coat and clean white breeches, anyone with any interest just assumed he was on some errand for someone in the upper echelons of the British command. The slave moved without confrontation through the main camp looking for a laundrywoman named Suzy.

He had never seen such activity. A train of wagons stretched from the docks at least a mile up the hill where it fanned out to provision the endless acres of tents, trenches, artillery stations, and support areas. Thousands of men, hundreds of women, and many children lent perpetual motion to the green fields.

James approached an attractive but disheveled thin woman in her midtwenties, Emily Corbin, who was carefully washing out an officer's fine shirt in a pan of soapy water.

James bowed respectfully and said, "Beg your pardon, but would you happen to know a laundress called Suzy?"

Emily cocked her head in thought for a few seconds and then said in a surprisingly refined accent, "I'm afraid no, but not to say there is no such. I know well the girls with whom I have traveled the campaign to date, but locals come and go, and she might well be one of those."

Like many other women, Emily had sailed with her husband, a newly enlisted private, from England to the American colonies. Women were shipped from the British Isles along with the British troops as an incentive for young men to join the army.

"Yes, missus, I see," James said. "I'll jest wander on then. Thank you for yo time."

"If she is not on the orderly's roll as belonging to a soldier as wife, she would receive no rations," Emily added. "Perhaps you would be best served to look near the sutlers. A girl might launder as a more commercial venture near there."

"I'm humbled by yo kindness, missus," James said.

He bowed again, backed away, and then walked toward the far edge of the encampment.

"Good luck," Emily called after him.

The women camp followers tended to laundering and mending clothing, cooking meals, and nursing the wounded. On the march, they were expected to keep up, often carrying pots and pans, personal belongings, and children as they struggled to keep pace in the dust behind the military columns. They led hard lives, being fully expected to earn their keep.

Emily sighed but thought to herself that, despite the hardships, army life was a vast improvement over the squalid slums of London, and perhaps the fighting would stop one day and she and her husband could settle into a good and peaceful life. Maybe even in this beautiful Virginia. She resumed rubbing at a tea stain on the fancy shirt.

James made his way to the fringe of the camp where the sutlers, vendors who followed the armies, had set up their makeshift stands. James noted alcohol, tobacco, paper, ham, bacon, coffee, and sugar for sale. He smiled to himself when he noted that most of the sutlers had the same gregarious, salesman-like personalities he had seen so often in the market at Williamsburg.

James ambled over to a man named Paul.

"Well, now!" Paul said. "You are obviously in the employ of a fine officer who demands only the finest table. May I suggest these robust cabbages?"

"They look mighty fine," James said, "but right now I lookin' for a young woman named Suzy who washes laundry."

Paul went into exaggerated deep thought and then asked, "Negro girl?"

"Yes, sir."

"She was run off," Paul shrugged. "Sassed an English officer. Lucky the girl was spared the lash."

No one else had any information about Suzy. Over an hour had passed, and James knew he had to get back. He thought maybe he could slip out at dark, somehow get to Williamsburg and Lafayette, and be back in Yorktown by sunup. He had no one else to trust and could not figure out another plan. He began walking back to the house when he heard a familiar voice. He stopped, scanned the tent city, and saw Nate singing to a group of British soldiers. A private had handed him the written lyrics, and the men were clapping along as Nate did a good job with the unfamiliar tune.

Come listen awhile and I'll tell you a song;
I'll show you those Yankees are all in the wrong,
Who, with blustering look and most awkward gait,
'Gainst their lawful sovereign dare for to prate,
With their hunting shirts and rifle guns.

Forgetting the mercies of Great Britain's King,
Who saved their forefathers' necks from the string,
With hunting shirts and rifle guns,
They renounce all allegiance and take up their arms,
Assemble together like hornets in swarms,
So dirty their backs, and so wretched their show,
That carrion-crow follows wherever they go,
With their hunting shirts and rifle guns.

Come take up your glasses, each true loyal heart,
And may every rebel meet his due desert,
With his hunting shirt and rifle gun.
May Congress, Conventions, those damned
inquisitions,
Be fed with hot sulphur from Lucifer's kitchens,
May commerce and peace again be restored,
And Americans own their true sovereign lord.

Then oblivion to shirts and rifle guns.
GOD SAVE THE KING!

The soldiers cheered and clapped, and a few of them offered Nate a farthing.

"No! No!" Nate insisted. "I sing for my love of the Crown! Now, if you fine and noble warriors were to purchase a portion of the finest dried corn in Virginia, I would not say no to that."

The boy passed through the soldiers with his basket of corn, and several of the men took some corn and pitched a coin into the basket.

Nate took a deep bow and said, "Thank you, kind sirs! Tomorrow I return with more music for your merriment and fine dried corn for your meal!"

He walked away from the smiling and waving redcoats. As Nate made his way over toward Milk, James took a path that would intercept the boy.

"Did you find her?" Emily walked up to James carrying two big bundles of freshly washed clothes.

"No, missus," James said as he looked over her shoulder at Nate moving further away. "I was told she got run off."

"She'll most likely turn up," Emily said. "Would you please help me with this? If I were to drop these shirts in the dirt and be faced with starting over, I would surely go mad."

"Well, missus, I . . ." Nate had reached Milk but was having a conversation with a spirit seller named Rummy-Jim. "Be pleased to. Where you goin'?"

"Just three or four rows over," Emily replied. "Won't take a minute."

James took one of the bundles in his arms and followed Emily through a row of tents, past a cooking pit, and then down another row. He looked back over his shoulder and caught a glimpse of Nate standing on a stump about to mount the horse. RummyJim remembered something and went back to Nate, so James had a little more time.

Emily and James reached a tent that was easily five times the size of the ones they had just passed. A major sat at a small mahogany table writing a letter. A servant stood ready to serve his needs.

Emily curtsied and said, "Your laundry, sir."

The major let out an exasperated sigh and made a curt motion to the servant, who rushed over and took the bundles from James and Emily.

"You are too well dressed to be a wash boy," the officer said to James. "For whom do you work?"

"That'd be His Excellency Lord Cornwallis, sir," James said and bowed slightly.

"Indeed!" The major exclaimed. He stood and snapped at Emily, "You will not waylay this man to ease your own burdens again, or I will make other arrangements for my shirts."

"Oh, yes, sir! I had no knowledge of his station with His Lordship. It will not happen ever again."

"Be off with you," the major said and sat back down to his writing.

Emily was having to practically run to keep up with James's fast pace. He craned his neck to try and catch a glimpse of Nate.

"Would you happen to know . . . by chance through an overheard exchange or such . . . how long we will be encamped here?" she asked as they cleared the tent rows.

"Lord, no, missus!" James replied. "I don't hear nothin' like that."

They stopped, and James saw that Nate and Milk were gone.

Emily said, "Could well be best to know nothing."

"Make life easier most'a the time," James said.

They parted amiably, and James spent the next few minutes trying to find Nate. Frustrated and despite the length of his absence, James sat down on a huge stump and tried to work out a plan. As he sometimes did when he needed to figure out something, the slave closed his eyes and rubbed his temples.

"You disappeared," Nate said.

The boy was sitting with his back to James's back on the wide stump.

"I saw you as I was singing and held hope we could talk. Does all go well?"

Neither man turned to look at the other as they conversed in hushed tones.

"I got news for General Lafayette," James said as he feigned interest in an escaped pig that was being chased through the area by three boys. "There s'posed to be others to take it on, but they can't."

"What can I do?" Nate asked under his breath.

"Get it to Williamsburg and the general if you can."

"I can. What is the message?"

"Cornwallis is thinkin' five thousand new troops from New York comin'. He also believe a Admiral Graves is sailin' nineteen ships here to take on what he sayin' is a few French ships."

"I understand," Nate whispered.

Before they separated, James said softly, "Rex got free, but . . ."

"He's free?!" Nate lit up. "Where is he?"

"I a'n't really got a way'a knowin', but I imagine he'll be findin' you fo it over wit."

"Or I him," Nate smiled.

Nate felt almost giddy with relief as he stood, walked a few feet, and sprung up onto Milk. Still smiling, Nate negotiated through the busy scene and on toward the Williamsburg road. Now that he knew Rex was safe, the boy was starting to feel excited about his mission and performing such a valuable service in the war.

James went a few yards before he walked around the side of a huge supply wagon and directly into Major Hiram Castellow. WHAP! Something struck James across the side of his head, and the big slave was knocked off balance. Major Castellow raised his riding crop again. His eyes were bloodshot and crazy, and he was clearly drunk. WHAP! He hit James again with the crop and then started pushing him in the general direction of the Nelson house.

"You'll twist in the wind for this," he said in a chilling tone.

Chapter 10

James shuffled along in a subservient way, but his mind was racing. He did not know for sure whether the major was furious at his absence or, worse, had overheard his conversation with Nate. The latter seemed unlikely, but men like Castellow were sneaky and had a gift for bearing witness to a man's vulnerability. James had to assume that Major Castellow had overheard at least part of what he had told Nate. His imagination was in overtime trying to come up with some innocent twist he could put on the conversation.

He also wondered what had become of Nate. Surely, he reasoned, if the major thought he was passing along classified information to the boy, Nate would be in custody. Perhaps he had been arrested. James knew that a slave and a farm boy would be treated differently no matter how common their offenses. James was scared, but he was also furious with himself. Caught on the very first day of his mission and possibly the reason his young friend would be imprisoned or worse. He focused every part of his brain on how to extricate himself from the situation and rescue Nate if need be.

*****

Nate rode on, unaware that his friend was in any trouble and thrilled that Rex was alive. He should have been tired and dreading the long ride back to Williamsburg, most of which would be done in the dark of night, but the adventure pumped him up, and he felt he would soon be reunited with his dog. The thousands of British soldiers in the camp amplified his feeling that he was going to be a part of something big and important. Tonight, he had information for General Lafayette, and he intended to deliver it. He could sleep when the war was over. Milk trundled on without protest.

*****

Rex was having a more difficult time. The long hours on the trail had inflamed his wounded foot, but he kept going. By the time he reached the familiar-scented Tyree plantation, the American soldiers were gone, and all was quiet. Rex smelled Nate, James, and his playmate Hannah all around the house but saw no one. Weak from his injuries, Rex lay down in the middle of the strongest Nate-scent he could find and went to sleep.

*****

As Major Castellow marched the slave back toward the Nelson house, the sun set and there was only a sliver of moon. In the dark, the major alternated swatting James with the crop every few steps with swilling from a small silver flask. By the time they reached Cornwallis's headquarters, he was weaving, falling down drunk.

"Youfh will rue ve day dath youfh crawfth pafths wif Mafor Hibam Cafellow," he slurred and raised the crop.

Before he could slam the weapon down on James's head again, the major fell over backwards and lay there motionless. That gave James a temporary reprieve. His options increased. With the major out cold, James could simply make a run for it. But running was not why he was in the war. There was a treasure trove of information in the Cornwallis compound, and something in the slave would not let him leave that intelligence behind.

At the Armistead house, James had witnessed the distorted memory that often comes with the next morning's hangover, so he decided to gamble. He would go inside and perform his duties as if nothing out of the ordinary had happened. Tomorrow, he would do the same. If Major Castellow remembered the evening's events and said anything, James would put on a blank, confused face and play dumb. He had observed at the Armistead house that men with hangovers remembered little that was taken seriously.

He straightened up his purple coat, squared his shoulders, and walked into the big house.

*****

Milk and Nate were only two miles from Yorktown when thick clouds blacked out the dim slice of moonlight. Nate had been in dark woods before, but nothing like this. He held his hand up in front of his face but could not see it. There was no light to reflect off of Milk's light-colored coat so the horse under him was like everything else, black nothing. Instinct kept the animal moving in the right direction, but the trip was surreal for the rider. He shielded his face from imaginary branches and all sorts of other obstacles that he could not see but expected. The night sounds he usually found comforting took on sinister proportions in his blindness.

Although Nate couldn't see it, an injured blue jay sat on a small fallen tree off to his right and slightly above his head. A thick three-foot snake sensed the heat of the bird and relentlessly inched his way up the downed trunk toward the blue jay.

"Yah!" Nate yelled out as several bats streaked out of nowhere and whizzed by his face.

He flung his arms around, and they struck the fallen tree hard. The bird went flying in one direction. The snake dropped onto Nate's shoulders and instinctively whipped itself around the panicking boy's face!

There was no up or down, no earth or sky, only total blackness and the horror of a scaly writhing snake around his neck, across his mouth, and over his eyes! Before he knew what was happening, the boy was on the ground rolling, screaming, pawing at the monster on his head! He grabbed the slithery whipping body with one hand and his knife with the other and began wildly stabbing at the serpent! He finally landed a jab and sliced with all of his might. The reptile twisted one last time and then went still.

"AAAAAH!"

Nate pulled the snake from his neck. The boy could feel blood running down the side of his head. His blade had deeply cut the snake and kept on going into his own skin. After he caught his breath and the shaking subsided, Nate ran his hands all over his skull. He felt two small puncture wounds by his right temple.

Nate attempted to stand but slumped back to the ground when a series of searing hot impulses shot from his head down through his arms and legs. The pain was intense. Even though it was a warm night, his teeth began to chatter. His mouth filled with foul-tasting bile, and he vomited.

"Merciful Lord," he moaned out loud. "Oh, Lord."

He could barely think what to do.

"Milk!" he called out weakly. "Milk!"

Nothing moved in the blackness. Milk was gone. Crawling along the ground, the only way Nate could negotiate the trail was to feel along the wagon tracks with his hands. The snake was dangling around his neck. At last, some moonlight came through the clouds. The first thing he did was look at the snake. A copperhead.

Nate remembered what his father had told him about the species that was common all over Virginia and encountered in brush, under ledges, and around wooden structures. There are two types of copperhead bites; neither is usually fatal to healthy people, but one is far worse than the other.

"It all depends," William had said, "on whether the snake is striking for defense or dinner."

If surprised, the copperhead went for a warning bite that contained very little venom. In feeding mode, the snake held on and pumped in as much venom as possible. Either attack was extremely painful and disorienting, but the former was relatively mild according to Nate's father. The boy could only hope that he had received the warning bite.

Even if that was the case, Nate had never felt worse. Still, the mission to Lafayette was hovering over him, and, so, after regurgitating some yellowish bile, he began walking, but it required tremendous effort.

"One foot forward," he concentrated. "Other foot forward."

His skin was red with flush, and looking down made him dizzy to the point of falling, but he trudged on.

As Nate got closer to Williamsburg, he was spotted by a posted American picket. The soldier was a farm boy himself, certainly saw no danger in Nate, and knew about the pain of a snakebite. The young picket was relieved a short time later and helped Nate stumble past other pickets and on to Williamsburg. He still felt horrible, but at least he knew he was not going to die.

*****

It was busy inside the Nelson house. Cornwallis had called a meeting with his top field officers. Hot scones and tea were being brought in from the kitchen to the preparation area outside the dining room. Henry made sure the tea was hot enough and artfully arranged the scones on a serving platter. James entered, and Henry cut him a disapproving look.

"I a'n't got time to dress you down for not bein' here. Take this into them officers, and I don't want to see you spill ary a crumb."

"Yes, Henry," James said.

He straightened his coat, picked up the platter, and walked into the dining room. Displayed on the long table were several maps and documents. Cornwallis sat at the head of the table, his second-in-command, General O'Hara, to his right. A dozen other high-ranking officers sat around the polished surface.

James set the platter on a side table and waited. The conversation seemed to center around the details of setting up the massive Yorktown camp. After a minute, Henry carried in the tea, and, with a nod toward Henry, O'Hara indicated that they could be served. The conversation continued as James and the older servant silently set out small plates, cups, and saucers in front of each man.

Before James could begin to pour the tea, the double doors leading to the entry hall flew open, and Castellow took an unsure step into the room. His eyes were beet red, and he was weaving where he stood. Eyebrows rose as every officer in the room knew the major was not only drunk but was also never included in meetings of any kind. Especially those lorded over by Cornwallis himself. The glare His Lordship leveled across the table at Castellow would have frozen a sober man with fear, but the major was far from sober.

Castellow moved his head slowly from left to right, squinting with concentration. Then he locked on James, who was at the far end of the table poised to pour Cornwallis his tea. The imposing nobleman was enraged by Castellow's intrusion and condition, but the only outward sign of his disgust was a slightly tightened upper lip and a minuscule tic in his cheek. O'Hara and the others knew the signs and went tense. Something bad was going to happen.

"Outside!" the major screamed at James and then lost his balance and had to grab the doorframe for support. "Youth about to receithe the beatink of youse life!"

"No," Cornwallis said evenly but in a tone so cold it sent chills up the younger officers' spines. "This man will now serve tea."

"Heeb insfolent and imcompement!" Castellow slurred.

"I see," Cornwallis replied. "Then you will serve the tea."

"Serb?"

"Now."

That one word came from the depths of a glacier and sounded like an edict from God. Everyone at the table stopped breathing.

The enormity of his dilemma began to seep through Castellow's drunken haze. He was scared, but there was no choice but to do what his superior had so forcefully dictated.

"Yeth, Your Lorpship," he said.

Touching the backs of the chairs for balance, he made his way to the head of the table and the tea service. James stepped back and stood next to the wall.

The major's hand was shaking so badly that he could barely hold the teapot level. Terrified of splashing tea on Cornwallis, he picked up the cup and saucer with his other hand. The china rattled in beat to the tremors in his hand.

"Your Eflency, I . . ."

The nobleman pointed to his cup, and Castellow tried. It was a humiliating performance. The tea came from the spout in a wiggly stream and splashed mainly into the saucer. Sweating now, Castellow stopped.

"Again," Cornwallis said.

The major gulped hard and set the cup and saucer on the table. Concentrating with all of his might, he held the teapot handle with both hands and tipped it forward. Some of the liquid hit the cup, but most of it went onto the table. In a pathetic gesture, Castellow wiped at the spill with the sleeve of his tunic.

"My alosogies, Your Lorbship, I . . ."

"Again."

Completely rattled now, the third attempt was worse. Castellow knocked the cup from the saucer with the tip of the teapot spout. Every officer at the table remained completely motionless, transfixed.

"Again."

What happened next was so demeaning that several of the officers had to look away. Castellow kneeled by the table and held the pot at eye level with both hands in his fourth attempt to pour the tea. It did not work. The tea missed the cup completely and seeped onto a map. Castellow hung his head and closed his eyes in shame.

"Again."

"I cannot oblige! I cannot oblige!" the major wailed and began to sob.

O'Hara nodded at a colonel, who stood up immediately and led a stumbling Castellow from the room.

"Let us continue, shall we?" Cornwallis said.

Castellow was never seen again. Some said he was in irons belowdecks on a ship in the harbor. Henry took over the kitchen, and it ran smoothly. James was given the position of first serve to Lord Cornwallis.

*****

William Tyree paced through the rooms of his plantation house. He had not slept well since the British forces had reached Virginia. The random terror and resupply raids by Tarleton and other guerrilla redcoats on outlying plantations were increasing in number and violence. He was sure that his decision to move his family into Williamsburg was the right choice.

It was early morning, dark, but the wagons were loaded. While some of Tyree's slaves had run off to join the British troops, five remained, and they saddled the horses and harnessed up the wagon teams. Mr. Tyree was ready to go. He woke his wife, and she, in turn, gently lifted a groggy Hannah from her bed and placed her on a big chair downstairs so a slave girl could pack Hannah's linens and blanket.

As her parents bustled around taking care of last-minute details, Hannah sleepily climbed down from the chair and wandered outside. Off to the side of the house, she saw Rex lying in a puddle of moonlight.

"The big dog!" she squealed. "You're back!"

Hannah was not Nate, but she was a friendly, familiar scent, and Rex greeted her with licks and a wagging tail. Her father was not keen on taking a huge dog with a wounded foot along, but Hannah unleashed such a dazzling display of questionable logic, flirty cuteness, and dramatic tears that the man gave in.

By morning, the family coach, two loaded wagons, the five slaves on horses, and Rex had traveled the almost twenty miles to Williamsburg.

*****

With the help of the young picket, an exhausted Nate made it to Williamsburg at about the same time as the Tyrees. He was practically asleep on his feet, but he made his way down Duke of Gloucester Street and across Market Square to Lafayette's headquarters. A sentry told him the general would not be in for at least two hours.

Ah, sleep. Nate walked over to the horse pens where he knew he could find a nice pile of hay to serve as a bed. As he approached the area, he saw several familiar faces including that of his horse.

"I should be mad at you," Nate smiled as he rubbed Milk's soft nose, "but between the snake and the darkness, I would have run myself had I the opportunity."

He settled down in the corner of the pen and went to sleep instantly.

An hour and a half later, the morning activity of the

troops woke the boy. As he rubbed his eyes and yawned, Sergeant Harrington walked up.

"Well, well," the big man said, "I was worried when Milk showed up alone, but I see you have managed to survive thus far."

"Thus far," Nate said and took the sergeant's extended hand.

As Harrington pulled Nate up to his feet, he said, "'Tis a nasty bite on your head there."

"Copperhead," Nate responded, wincing "It's throbbing mightily."

"This way," the sergeant said and Nate followed him to a medical tent.

Harrington left him with a corporal who applied a poultice made of milk, bread, and salad oil to Nate's head and gave him some water gruel with vinegar to eat, assuring him that it was part of the treatment. It had been only a short nap, but, now, with a little rest and feeling a bit better, Nate felt anxious to get back on the job. He went back to Lafayette's headquarters.

"*Excellent!*" the French general exclaimed when Nate passed on the information about the British fleet and the enemy's belief that only a few French ships were en route to help the patriots. "We'll not know for sure until Admiral de Grasse actually arrives, but we are in hopes that he is sailing north from the West Indies with perhaps as many as forty heavily armed *navires*."

"So, there would be a big sea battle?" Nate asked.

"*Oui. Entre nous,* if we control the water lanes and General Washington brings down his forces from New York to seal off the land routes, Cornwallis has nowhere to run."

Nate thought a few seconds and then said, "A rat in a trap."

"Précisément," Lafayette said and smiled.

A few blocks over, the Tyrees were getting settled in a rented house on England Street. The slaves were emptying the wagons under Mrs. Tyree's directions. Before they left to do some errands on Duke of Gloucester Street, William and Hannah tied Rex to the front fence.

"We'll find some liniment for the dog's foot," William said.

"You be a good doggie," Hannah said, and she left with her father.

Rex's eyes followed them the half block up to busy Duke of Gloucester Street. He sat down and watched the various carts, coaches, animals, and pedestrians come and go.

Rex's foot injury was sapping his strength. Sleep was the only thing that gave him relief from the pain, but, before he could settle down onto the grass, a boy on a light-colored draft horse trotted through his field of vision. Nate was leaving for Yorktown. General Lafayette had been pleased with the intelligence, the boy's headache from the snakebite was gone, and he felt on top of the world. Pumped up with excitement, he urged Milk into a trot.

The big dog was not sleepy any more. Nate! At the precise moment he let loose his loudest bark, three cannons, part of a medal ceremony on the green, fired. The boy on the horse did not hear the bark and passed out of the dog's window of sight.

Rex strained against the rope, but it was securely tied to the picket fence. Not to be kept from his master any longer, he simply lunged, and his massive, muscular weight snapped the thin wooden fence slat like a matchstick. Trailing several feet of rope, Rex broke into a lumbering three-legged half run. He reached the busy street and turned left. Pedestrians scattered as the huge animal careened along like a runaway stagecoach. Rex caught sight of Nate near the end of the street and raced on.

Frantic and with a desperate whine in his throat, Rex bolted around and through the maze of oxen and horse legs that clogged the street. Suddenly, a clear opening! He would make it! And then . . .

THHHWAP! His rope had somehow become entwined in the wheels of a carriage! The spinning motion of the wheel wound up the rope like a spool of thread and slammed Rex into the hub. BAP! BAP! BAP! Around he went, slamming into the ground with each turn of the tall wheel.

The passenger in the carriage leaned out as the coachman pulled up the team of horses. People gathered around, gawking. A big man in a buckskin shirt cut the rope from the wheel with a huge knife. A woman with gentle eyes kneeled by the motionless Rex and slipped the rope from around his neck.

"He's still breathing," she said.

"Stupid animal!" shouted the dandy owner of the carriage. "Two of my spokes are broken!"

Rex opened his eyes, stood, and pushed his way past the kind woman.

"Oh, my!" she said as he stumbled toward the end of the street.

There was a lot of activity down near the old Capitol, but not a boy on a draft horse in sight.

Moving like a sick old man with bad legs, Rex went looking for his master.

CHAPTER 11

There was a garrison of Continental troops on the Capitol lawn. A stooped man, Thomas, barefoot and dressed in a stain-covered shirt and baggy pants held up by a greasy piece of rope, was collecting trash from the camp in a one-horse cart. His load was huge. The mountain of refuse in the narrow vehicle seemed destined to topple over at any second. And yet, he piled on more. The cart stopped at a cooking pit, and Thomas shoveled a mound of blackened debris onto his teetering cargo.

"Ye've outdone yourself, today, Thomas," a cook laughed. "I'll wager a shilling ye'll not go past quarter of a mile 'fore the whole kit comes a'tumblin' down."

"Have your shillin' ready for me on the morrow," Thomas grinned. "'Tis a true prodigy in the art of balance I am."

The cook chuckled, shook his head with wonder, and went back to work. Thomas took one last look at his masterpiece, seemed satisfied, and climbed up onto the driver seat. He clucked at his horse, and the cart began to move. Even with the added weight of a very big dog that had dragged himself onto the rear of the cart, not a single thing fell off. There was still Nate-scent in the air when the cart turned onto the road to Yorktown.

Traffic on the road just outside of Williamsburg was steady as a few farmers brought to market what produce and livestock had escaped the British. Nate recognized three of the farmers, but he was in a hurry and only gave them a friendly nod. He did not have time to stop and chat about the weather and war. He had little choice, however, when Captain Rawlinson spotted him and trotted over on his horse.

"Greetings, young Chandler!" the young captain said. "From what I hear, you've put quite a feather in my cap!"

"Good morning, sir," Nate said. "A feather?"

"Yes, indeed! 'Twas I who brought you to the camp, and, even though I deserve no credit in the matter whatsoever, your heroics reflect kindly on my judgment."

"I've done no heroics, sir."

"Nonsense. Now, I insist you regale me with all of your latest exploits. Here, we'll share this small buttermilk cake I just received from my sister."

"Really, sir, I . . ."

Rawlinson tore the small cake in half, handed Nate a piece, and hooked his leg up over his saddle in a relaxed position for conversation.

"Yorktown will be there when you arrive. Now, tell me an adventure."

Nate did not think he should go into much about his spying out here on the open road so he said, "Well, sir, there was this snake . . ."

Fifteen minutes later, Nate was more than ready to continue his trip, but Rawlinson seemed content to wile away the morning. During a brief lull, Nate decided his only escape lay in name-dropping.

"It's been grand seeing you, sir," he said, "but, as General Lafayette told me in our private meeting this very morning, there are priorities involved with war. I really must take my leave of you."

"I . . . see. Of course," the captain said.

They clapped each other on the shoulder, and Rawlinson galloped away toward Williamsburg. Nate hesitated a few seconds to let pass a cart stacked with what he thought was surely the tallest pile of trash he had ever seen. As the cart passed him, Nate looked into the blue eyes of his dog.

A loud BARK!

"Rex!"

Thomas never knew that the dog had hitched a ride or that a farm boy had lifted the animal from the back of his conveyance. Sheer excitement overrode Rex's injuries, and he covered Nate in slobbery licks. The boy hugged the big animal, scratched his ears, and talked to him like a long-lost brother. When the initial joy subsided, Nate noticed the foot and coach wheel wounds.

"You've had a tough time of it, old boy," he said. "But I'll have you bounding around in no time."

Bounding or not, Rex looked content as he lay across Milk in front of his master as the three of them returned to Yorktown and a brewing battle. They reached the abandoned farmhouse a few hours later. During the next days, Nate bartered some of his corn for a medicinal solution from a British medical officer and a variety of herb concoctions from a strange "healer" who wandered around the camp.

The dog's inflamed foot was the most serious injury, but ticks were not helping the cuts and scrapes Rex had received from Adickes. During his treks through the woods, dozens of the bloodsuckers had attached themselves to the open wounds. Some of the ticks were fat with blood and visible. Nate picked those off and burned them with a glowing stick from the fire. They were so engorged that the vampire insects popped like little firecrackers when touched by the flame.

Other ticks had worked themselves deeper into Rex's cuts. RummyJim claimed rum would clear up the problem. With no better idea, Nate held the dog steady with his legs and poured a small amount of rum from the sutler into the open sores. Rex squealed and squirmed, but the elixir was too much for the ticks and, after three treatments, the wounds were healing nicely.

Nate disguised the smelly herb mixture from the healer in some sweetened corn mush and fed it to his dog twice a day. Something in the concoction worked as Rex's foot was in good shape in less than a week.

Using the leather from an old bridle he found on the farm, Nate made Rex a new collar. He thought about scratching his name on it, but, considering his present line of work, decided against the idea.

Like almost every other enterprise, spying took on elements of routine after a while. Nate and Rex would go into the British camp in the morning with the basket of corn. Sentries were in place, but they recognized the boy and his dog and waved them through without incident. They were expected now, and the soldiers looked forward to the boy's corn and amusing songs.

Nate began one of their favorites:

O can't you see yon little turtle dove
Sitting under the mulberry tree?
See how that she doth mourn for her true love:

And I shall mourn for thee, my dear,
And I shall mourn for thee.

O fare thee well, my little turtle dove,
And fare thee well for a-while;
But though I go I'll surely come again,
If I go ten thousand mile, my dear,
If I go ten thousand mile.

Nate's little show provided some relief from a soldier's greatest burden—boredom. The boy's outgoing personality was an unusual but welcome spark in the lives of the mostly stoic Englishmen.

"Liven up, lads!" he would joke as he approached a group of soldiers. "Why, I've seen lumps on a log with brighter faces! Not to fret, you'll have your battle with the rebels soon enough. Sing along with me!"

On at least two occasions, Nate was singing when Lord Cornwallis himself happened by during the course of camp inspections. The dour-faced nobleman made no comment but did not tell the boy to stop.

Nate sat at their fires, did some odd jobs for the soldiers, and joined an occasional meal. Some of the men gave Rex scraps and even threw a stick for him to retrieve, an exercise that the soldiers, as they did with practically everything else, turned into a game of chance.

"A farthing the dog takes fourteen or less steps to bring back the stick," one said.

"A wager I accept!" said another. "The animal will require fifteen or more if he needs but one."

Everyone was comfortable with the farm boy and his dog. After only a week, Nate and Rex were a part of the daily camp scene, and no one gave a second thought to their presence.

What the troops did not know was that as he sang and joked and sold his corn, Nate was counting everything: the number of troops, cannons, cannonballs, muskets, musket ball boxes, gunpowder stores, food provisions, sick soldiers, mercenaries, supply wagons, horses, and on and on. To keep track, he used a corn kernel to designate ten of whatever he was counting.

James was simultaneously eavesdropping on Lord Cornwallis and his discussions of strategy with his staff. Since the incident with the drunken Major Castellow, James was elevated in the household. Everyone referred to him as "His Lordship's man" as Cornwallis was perfectly pleased with the slave's serving skills, demeanor, and deference. Cornwallis and his staff openly talked of military matters at meals as if James were no more than a piece of furniture in a corner.

In late August, O'Hara said, "We are perplexed by General Washington," to the dinner group as Lord Cornwallis looked on. "His main army is marching south from New York, but surely no destination past New Jersey comprises his plan."

"Would there be a chance the armies are coming to Virginia?" a colonel asked.

"No," Cornwallis said, but with concern in his voice.

His concerns were warranted.

In early August, Washington had learned that French Admiral de Grasse had set sail from the West Indies with a large armada and was heading for the Chesapeake Bay. That made it clear to the general that his troops must be moved from New York to Virginia. If de Grasse could seal off the harbor and Washington's troops could cut off lines of escape by land, Cornwallis would be trapped. But how to move the fourteen thousand American and French forces from New York all the way to Virginia without alerting British General Clinton, who would undoubtedly stage some kind of delaying action?

Deception. Make it look like the Continental army was preparing to retake New York City from the British. American attack landing craft were set out so they could be seen by the British lookouts. Roads to New York City were repaired. Giant bake ovens were built to make it appear that the army was going to feed many troops for a long time in the area. On August 26, the French-American army moved out, made a false feint toward New York, and then began its 450-mile trek to Virginia.

The trickery worked. By the time Clinton realized the Continental troops were moving south, they were already too far for him to do anything about it.

The unknown strength of the approaching French fleet also seemed to confuse the generals. James was no military strategist, but he could read people, and, to him, it looked as though the mighty British army was getting nervous. Nate sensed the same thing in officers out in the camp and passed along the observation to Lafayette along with the other intelligence he and James gathered on an almost daily basis.

One aspect of the spy game that had become relatively routine was the transference of information. Every afternoon, James would go to the camps to obtain the best produce and meat for Lord Cornwallis. When he had something to tell Nate, the slave hung a small handkerchief in the lapel pocket of his coat. If the boy spotted the handkerchief, he would eventually wander over near James. After a few minutes, the two would walk for a short distance as James relayed what he had learned in the dining room. That intelligence along with the numbers, gossip, and observations Nate gathered was delivered to Lafayette in Williamsburg at the boy's discretion. Sometimes, it made sense to wait a few days if the information was not critical. At other times, it needed to be passed on to the French general immediately.

When Nate said "Lafayette," Rex knew they would be going to Williamsburg. Nate took along a pitch-tar torch to light their way through the night. After the first couple of trips, there were few pickets, British or American, who did not recognize the boy, his big dog, and his bigger horse. They were occasionally stopped, but Nate knew the game now and had his innocent farmer routine down cold. It always worked, and they were waved through. They were usually back in Yorktown, singing and selling corn, by midmorning of the next day.

Chapter 12

The camp followers—sutlers, traders, and other non-military cooks, laundresses, scavengers, and diggers—formed a loose fraternity. They saw each other every day, and each had his or her role and turf. There was little friction among them, and many became friends. Nate often joked around with RummyJim, whose niche in the operation was simple: he sold rum and other liquor. No one was quite sure how he got the goods, but he seemed to have a never-ending supply.

RummyJim sampled his wares often, which probably contributed to his slightly off-center stance, gravely voice, and beetlike nose. There was no explanation for his bright purple velvet greatcoat, yellow hat, and red boots.

"God bless me!" RummyJim bellowed. "'Tis the corn dog and his cherub little master looking lively as crickets this fine morning!"

"Well, I sing my songs and sell my corn," Nate laughed.

"He who cannot do as he would must do what he can."

"Ha! And RummyJim knows what I would do?"

RummyJim threw back his head and laughed.

"Aye! Like all lads, you are head over ears to go to sea."

"I harbor no such inclination. I hear the sea can be a rough mistress, and, for truth, I do not want to drown in her arms."

"He who is born to be hanged will never be drowned."

"Time will tell which of us goes first to the gallows."

RummyJim laughed.

"Come along, ragamuffins. RummyJim has deliveries in the bay and needs your strong back and cheerful countenance to carry out the task."

"I must desire that you change the subject, for I have not the slightest thoughts of going," responded Nate.

"Not for a guinea?"

"A real guinea?!"

"All you need do is help a feeble old man load some barrels."

"Feeble? Ha! Where might these barrels be and where are they going?"

Ten minutes later, RummyJim and Nate were loading kegs of rum onto a small, sturdy, single-masted work boat.

"Four British ships out at the mouth of the bay," RummyJim said. "The lads are thirsty, and it is my duty to wet their whistles! Sail ho!"

Being on a boat was unfamiliar to Rex, but he sniffed around and seemed ready for the adventure. Then they cast off and began plowing through the choppy water. Rex fell several times but eventually got his footing. It wasn't long before the dog was standing at the bow, his face happily in the wind and spray. Nate had never been out in big water in a boat either, and it took a while longer for Nate's sea legs to settle in and adjust to the rolling motion of the craft. After minimal instruction, he held the tiller for RummyJim.

It took two and a half hours to sail the five miles out to the spot where the York River merged with the ten-mile-wide Chesapeake Bay. Four British ships came into view. As RummyJim pulled the small boat up next to the frigate anchored furthest out, a sailor threw down a line.

"Some time past, you was kind enough to sell me a gracious quantity of your rum," the sailor said as RummyJim climbed a rope ladder up to the deck. "I'm not alone in the hope you bring replacement for the elixir, which has, alas, run dry. Should you be able to comply, I would be your servant, sir."

"Sir, I am yours," RummyJim said with a bow. "Let no man sleep this night without his stomach be full of the finest rum this side of Barbados!"

That ship alone hoisted up seven barrels of rum from the deck of the small boat. As Nate rolled the containers into the net, he thought that maybe, if RummyJim were allowed to refresh the entire British military, there might not be much fight left in them when the time came.

An amiable supplier and not one to just take the money and run, RummyJim sat up on deck with the officers and sailors telling tall tales. With three ships to go, Nate saw that this might take all day. Still, there was no spy intelligence to deliver today, and, in a time when hard coinage was all but impossible to obtain, a guinea was a guinea. He settled down by the tiller and looked out to sea. After a few seconds, he squinted and rubbed his eyes. Then he looked again. The two-mile-wide row of white sails was still there and coming their way. All of them were flying French colors.

"This changes everything," Nate whispered to himself.

The laughter from up on the deck continued. How could they not see that many ships on the horizon? They would see them soon, but Nate intended to be on the way to Williamsburg and Lafayette before that happened. He slipped the line from the boat and pushed away with all of his might, but it was not enough. Something about the motion of the bigger boat at anchor seemed to suck the smaller craft to its side. Nate picked up a long oar, placed it against the hull of the frigate, and pushed with all of his might. The little boat moved out and, once a few feet from the big hull, floated free.

"Ships ahoy! Ships ahoy!" rang out from high in the rigging of the frigate.

Nate could hear a lot of feet running up on deck and loud yelps and calls. They will be looking the other way, out to sea at the French fleet, he thought, but not for long.

When they left Yorktown, Nate had helped Rummy-Jim pull a line and the sail went up, but which one? He yanked on one line, but nothing happened. Which one?! BAM! The small boat drifted back into the side of the frigate. Nate fully expected some bellowing from RummyJim at that instant, but no one was looking. RummyJim and all of the officers and crew of the ship were standing open-mouthed at the opposite rail looking in disbelief at the French ship–filled horizon.

Nate pushed away again with the oar and then tugged on three lines at once. One of them engaged, and the sail started inching up the mast. Pull! Pull! At last, the sail was up, and Nate tied the line to a heavy wooden cleat. The untended rudder was flopping around when the wind caught the sail, and the craft blew over at a perilous angle. Rex was sliding around on the wet deck fighting for footing as Nate scrambled back to the stern and grabbed the tiller. He moved it back and forth until the boat seemed to settle down suddenly and plane over the choppy bay.

There was nothing pretty about the way he sailed away, but he got the vessel headed in the right direction and held on. They were a hundred yards away before the rum merchant's bullhorn-like obscenities reverberated across the water.

"My apologies!" Nate yelled out, but his voice was lost in the wind.

Rex took bowsprit duty and barked incessantly as the little craft rose and fell as it left the bay and sailed through the increasingly rough waters of the wide and very deep York River. Nate certainly had no technical sailing skills, but there was a feel to the way the boat responded to the tiller. He found as long as he kept the tiller steady at a place where the boat was kind of leaning into the wind, the sails stayed full, and rapid progress was made. If he turned the tiller the other way, the sail began to flop, and he was in danger of coming to a stop. RummyJim had occasionally done things to adjust the sail, but Nate knew nothing of that. Nonetheless, he figured that, since he was moving in the right direction, he would just hang on and hope for the best.

Soon after they entered the waters of the York River and were approaching Yorktown, dark clouds rolled in quickly, and a powerful wind swept across the river. The chops on the water were now full-fledged waves with foamy whitecaps. Nate did not know to trim the sail, and the canvas was stretched to bursting. The little boat plowed and surfed through the pounding water at full speed. It was a rough ride, and Rex was being tossed around like a doll.

Holding onto the tiller with all of his might, Nate shouted, "Hang on, Rex! Hang on!"

Although it was basically out of control, the boat had so much speed that they passed by Yorktown in only minutes. Eyes narrowed through the spray and wind, Nate kept the craft pointed generally west toward Williamsburg. That task became even more difficult as a thick fog descended and lay right on top of the river's surface. It was not unusual for such a fog to appear almost instantly and out of nowhere in this area where river met bay.

Nate now concentrated on not crashing into the shoreline, but he might as well have been wearing a blindfold. A gale-force gust shot the boat over two breaking waves into an even denser fog, and CRASH! Whatever they hit was solid, and the force of the sudden stop sent both Rex and Nate spinning overboard and into the choppy water. Nate's head broke up through the waves. Even though he had mastered gliding through the small stream back at the farm, staying afloat and alive in this was a totally different exercise. Very few people in colonial America could actually swim, and Nate was no exception. He tried to call out for Rex, but a wave broke into his mouth, and he gagged and flailed until a rum barrel popped up right in front of him.

He wrapped his arms around the barrel and held on. The effort was draining the boy, and he knew he would soon go under for good. An image of his family sitting by a warm fire in their farmhouse came into his head as his grip loosened on the barrel and he slid under the surface.

"Yah! Look there!" someone shouted.

Then something came through the water, snaked its way under Nate's arms, and yanked him backwards and up onto something solid. He was on the deck of a barge being used to transport dragoons and their horses across the river to their camp outside Gloucester Point. Their barge was so big and heavy that it plowed along through the rough waves and whipping wind at a reasonably stable attitude.

Nate coughed up what seemed like gallons of water before he was able to sit up and look around. All he could see through the fog were the shadowy shapes of men and horses. Then a strong hand grabbed his neck and slammed him back down to the deck. He looked up into the ferocious eyes of Sergeant Clinton Adickes.

"I know this boy," Adickes sneered through his greenish teeth. "Cut my leg with a blade, he did."

He squeezed tighter on Nate's neck.

"No man draws the blood of Clinton Adickes and sees the deed unpunished."

"Heathen criminal!" Nate managed to gasp. His eyes were blazing with hate.

Adickes laughed, kneeled on his chest, and looped a rope around his ankles.

"Scrum for the fishes," he snorted and pitched Nate off the back of the barge.

Chapter 13

The barge was moving slowly, but there was enough forward motion to force briny water into his mouth and nose, and Nate was drowning. Desperate to free himself from the rope, he felt for his knife, but it was gone. Suddenly, the barge hit a big rogue wave that pushed the vessel back toward Nate a few feet, creating some slack in the rope. Nate frantically tugged at it. He couldn't get it off. Running out of breath, tied up and suffocating, the boy felt absolute panic. Seconds before he would have lost consciousness, he worked the rope free and kicked desperately for the surface.

His first breath was the best thing Nate had ever felt. But, then, he could see that the horror was not over. They were close to the Gloucester side of the river, the storm was subsiding, and the fog was lifting. One light puff of wind and the dragoons would see him adrift and alive. He knew he had to go back under. As he floundered in the water, his legs kicked the branch of a submerged tree. He grabbed the branch, took the deepest of breaths, and forced himself back under.

"Let us have a look at our piggy on a string," Sergeant Adickes snarled as he began pulling in the rope. "If he still kicks, back in he goes!"

The line came in too easily, and there was nothing but an empty loop on its end.

"Argh," the sergeant said.

He moved his gaze slowly across the surface of the now-visible water. For half a minute, he scanned the waves for some sign of Nate.

The boy reached his limit just as Adickes said, "Dead as a crab," with great glee. Still clutching the limb, Nate pushed his head through the surface of the water, resigned to whatever fate lay in wait.

At the precise second his head broke the water, a dragoon infantryman shouted, "Sergeant! Look! The gods of the sea have blessed us mightily and sure!"

Adickes jerked his head toward the shore and saw twenty-two barrels of rum rolling in the surf.

"Huzzah and glory be!" he shouted. "In ye go, lads! Spill not a drop!"

Cheering, the dragoons jumped from the barge into the shallow water and began merrily rescuing the barrels. The cavalrymen were completely focused on getting the treasure back to their camp safely, and not a one of them so much as glanced back out over the river. For the fifteen minutes it took the soldiers to unload their horses, pack up the rum, and disappear up the trail, Nate remained as low and still in the water as possible.

The last dragoon faded from sight, and Nate splashed and flailed a few feet from the safety of the tree before he reached water shallow enough so that he could stand. He waded in to shore and collapsed next to a big pine tree.

*****

Across the river on the Yorktown side, Rex splashed through the last few feet of water and up onto dry land. After the collision, he had spent a long time swimming in circles looking for Nate, but, at last, he had followed his nose through the fog and past the few ships anchored off Yorktown. The fog had not lifted on that side of the river, so Rex just sat down and waited for his master to walk through the haze. Even after the fog lifted, there was still no Nate, but the dog stayed put, looking out at the river.

There was a lot of activity up the hill at Lord Cornwallis's headquarters. The French fleet had been sighted. It was fully twice as large as expected and, worse, exceeded the number of ships British Admiral Graves had dispatched to Yorktown. Sketchy intelligence had several of the French vessels unloading thousands of troops at a landing on the parallel James River. It did not look good, but James was impressed by the unflappable demeanor of Cornwallis. The veteran soldier digested each piece of information, weighed its importance, and gave decisive orders.

Cornwallis dispatched two officers down to the riverfront to scout out a less vulnerable headquarters site than the exposed hilltop Nelson house.

"Why would such a move be necessary, sir?" a captain asked.

"Because," Cornwallis said without a trace of emotion, "it will soon be raining cannonballs."

Henry sent James down to the waterfront to see if there was fresh fish available for Cornwallis's table. The busy area was buzzing with talk of the French ships. Before the slave could look for a fishmonger, he spotted Rex sitting forlornly by the water.

"What you doin' out here, boy?" James asked, surprised, as he walked up.

Rex greeted him with a wagging tail and a lick or two.

"Where's yo master?"

"That mongrel been sitting out here for hours," a craggy fisherman said. "Mean dog. I gave hearty attempt at running him off, but growls and a snarly lip were my reward."

"Oh, this ole thing a'n't mean. He's jest lookin' for a lad. You seen a boy? Farm lad with a felt hat?"

"Nope. Now, move on with you, and take the beast."

"Off we go," James said and took Rex by the collar.

He had to almost drag the dog for the first few feet.

"We'll find Nate. Don't you concern yourself about it. Come on, now."

Rex relaxed some and walked with the slave. Every few yards, the dog would look back at the river.

"Mercy," James mumbled under his breath, "where did that boy go off to now?"

*****

After Nate rested, he spent an hour scouring the Gloucester-side shoreline for some sign of his dog, but there was nothing. Rage was building in the boy. For the past few weeks, he had been so occupied with spying that the horrible wounds to his parents and destruction of their home had been pushed to the back of his mind. The trauma was still there, of course, but having something important to do busied his mind. But, now his dog had drowned, and the rest came rushing back.

The dragoon sergeant. He was responsible for everything! Nate knew that the information about the French fleet was all-important. He knew that piece of intelligence could swing the momentum of the war. He knew General Lafayette was poised, waiting for just such news. He knew all of that, but he could not proceed until he took care of something. He was not going anywhere or doing anything until he killed a man.

The rum was not going to waste. Colonel Tarleton was in Yorktown with Cornwallis, so the cavalrymen were making the most of Sergeant Adickes's order to "wind it up a bit." Barrels were tapped, and, by early evening, there was not a sober breath being drawn by any member of the Virginia contingent of His Majesty's Royal Dragoons. Nate watched the singing, wrestling, and general foolishness from his perch high up in an ancient oak tree.

By nightfall, the few men left standing, Sergeant Adickes among them, raised one last toast and staggered off to collapse on their bunks. Nate eased down the tree, past the one snoring sentry, and into the camp. He walked past the dying fire and into Adickes's tent.

*****

Cornwallis's headquarters was dimly lit by a few candles as James and Rex trudged back up the hill. A staff meeting was in progress.

After the French ships were spotted, the pressure on the British command increased. Cornwallis and his staff were discussing strategy. One suggestion was to dispense false information to Lafayette to perhaps improve the British hand. The redcoat officers assumed that the Americans would tighten and increase security measures and road checks, so sending a British officer, no matter how cleverly disguised, to plant a document with Lafayette would be a gamble.

“Perhaps we could send a trusted sutler or servant under some ruse,” a colonel suggested.

“There are no trusted sutlers,” O’Hara injected, “and what servant would not bungle the plan?”

“Send my man, James,” Cornwallis said. “He will do it quite well.”

“Are you sure, Your Lordship?” O’Hara asked. “Surely we can disguise a private or sergeant who would . . .”

“James,” Cornwallis said with finality. “Now.”

The discussion was over.

O’Hara, followed by Captain Tompkins, left the room, sent for James, and began dictating a letter to Tompkins in Cornwallis’s office.

“Step here,” General O’Hara said to James as he entered the hallway. “His Lordship has an important bit of, shall we say, trickery that he believes you are qualified to execute.”

“My mama told me once that, if she had it to do over, she’a named me Trickery.”

“Indeed,” the humorless general sniffed.

Captain Tompkins finished the letter and handed it to O’Hara, who read it and nodded approval. The captain applied a pressed seal to the lower right-hand corner of the high-quality paper. Then, to James’s surprise, Tompkins balled up the document, dropped it on the floor, and ground some mud from his boot into it.

“Lord, sir!” James exclaimed.

The captain picked up the document and handed it to James.

“Stuff that into your pocket,” he said.

“Yes, sir, I’ll stuff it in this pocket here, but I don’t know what to do wit it past that.”

"You'll deliver it to General Lafayette in Williamsburg," O'Hara said.

"Beg yo pardon, general, sir, but I think slow-headed James has missed sumpin' here."

"It's false information," O'Hara said. "In the course of your duties, you found it mistakenly discarded and, being a patriot at heart, you felt the general might find it to be of some use."

"Hmm," James said after a moment's thought. "So they reads sumpin' which a'n't quite right and makes some kind'a move or other cause'a that and whatever they does is wrong and then the fine British army can jest jump up and down all over whatever it is that they done cause they read sumpin' they thought was from you and it was cept it was all twisted like."

"He's smarter than he looks," Tompkins said to O'Hara.

"A matter of opinion," the general shot back and left the office to return to the meeting.

"You understand your story?" the captain asked.

"Yes, sir. I was jest sweeping up and I seed that fine paper with His Lordship's seal on it, see, and so I say to myself . . ."

Captain Tompkins raised his hand for silence and said, "Go."

"I'll go on down the road then."

Rex was waiting out front when James exited the house.

"Rex, we're goin' to see General Lafayette."

James knew that accurate information regarding the arrival of French ships would be very important to the French general and perhaps even the war's outcome.

Rex associated the word "Lafayette" with a treat, and he led the way toward the road to Williamsburg.

*****

Nate had never been in a cave full of sleeping bears, but he was sure that snoring would not have been worse than the symphony coming from Adickes and his three tentmates. The boy was strangely calm as he looked down at the open-mouthed rat face of the man he held responsible for his parents' grave injuries, the destruction of his home, and now the drowning of his dog. In their drunken state, none of the men had removed their boots or scabbards. Without emotion, Nate eased Adickes's own dagger from the sergeant's belt.

*****

James had gone barefoot much of his life. When he had serious walking to do, he removed his shoes since none were remotely as comfortable as his bare feet. He was especially glad to shed the hard buckled shoes that were part of his server uniform. Unencumbered by those, James and Rex set a fast pace along the dark road.

The soles of the slave's feet were covered in a layer of callus thicker and tougher than any leather, but even they were no match for a butcher's hook. The wickedly sharp instrument had bounced from a cart earlier in the day and become wedged, point up, in a piece of shale by the trail. James stumbled on something in the dark and landed on the hook. His full weight drove the sharp metal through the thick callus, past muscle and bone, and out the top of his right foot.

"YAAAAAAA!"

The pain was intense. The slave hopped for a few feet and then fell to the ground.

"Lord almighty! YEEEEEEEE!"

Gasping for breath and with tears of pain streaming down his face, James lifted the wounded foot, grabbed the hook on the sole side of his foot, and did what he had to do. He pulled it all the way back through and out.

"Sweet Jesus! Jesus, Jesus, Jesus! Oh, Lord! Arrrrrgh!"

The hook fell to the side, and James flopped over backwards. He lay there a minute, hyperventilating and moaning.

Rex stood close. After a bit, James sat up and tried to stand but could not. He might stumble his way back the mile or two to Yorktown and get some aid, but there was no way he could walk the twelve miles to Williamsburg. He sat down again and wrapped his handkerchief around the injured foot. It was bleeding steadily, and the pain was getting worse. He tried to think. He had to get the information to Lafayette.

"Let's see, now, let's see," he said and tried to figure out a plan.

A few minutes later, James had the crumpled up misinformation document from Captain Tompkins flattened out on a smooth stump. He dipped a sharp-ended stick into a small pool of his own blood and drew a big "X" across the captain's words and the seal of Lord Cornwallis. He fanned it in the night air to dry the blood. Then he turned the paper over and drew the Yorktown coastline to the best of his recollection. He drew twenty-eight sails formed around a French flag at the mouth of the Chesapeake Bay. North of that, he drew a British flag and eighteen sails. He blew on the blood, and it dried quickly.

"Well, that's 'bout all I know to do," he said to Rex.

James folded the paper carefully and placed it in a little pouch he made from his bandana. He laced the long ends of the pouch around the dog's collar and tied them securely.

"Up to you now, boy," he said and motioned for the dog to get going.

Rex sat still.

"Lafayette," James said. "Take it to Lafayette."

Rex took some steps down the road but stopped.

"Lafayette!" James shouted. "Lafayette! Go on, now!"

Rex turned and ran off in the direction of Williamsburg. The route was so familiar now that the trip was instinctive. At a loping ten miles an hour, the dog was on Duke of Gloucester Street by eleven in the evening. He went directly to Lafayette's headquarters, a route he had repeated with Nate at least a dozen times over the past weeks. All he had to do now was enter the house, walk down a center hall, go into the last room on the left, and wait for his molasses cakes. The general had made the mistake of offhandedly pitching one of the treats to Rex as he received information from Nate on one of the pair's first trips from Yorktown. From that moment on, whenever the dog was in proximity to Lafayette, he would look up at him with pitiful doe eyes and sniff at the general's pockets until a molasses cake was produced. It amused the general, and he liked Rex.

But, now there was a problem. Some new members of the Virginia militia had recently come to Williamsburg, and part of their assignment was to guard command headquarters. While the usual sentries all knew Rex, the new private was not about to let a giant dog with a bloody bandana around his neck just wander into General Lafayette's office.

"Off with you, dog!" the guard shouted at Rex as he tried to negotiate his way past the front door and on to his treat.

He grabbed the dog's collar through the bandana cloth and tried to pull him away from the house.

"This dang dog is strong as a bull!" exclaimed the guard, giving up on trying to physically move Rex. "Git! I'll kick the fire out'a you if you don't git!"

Rex tried to dart by the man once, but the guard landed a swift kick and then drew his saber.

"I don't wanna kill no dog, but I shore will! Now, git on with you!"

Rex looked at the wild-eyed soldier and got the message. He turned and walked off into the dark.

"And stay gone!" rang out the soldier's voice.

Rex was thirsty, and a short nap wouldn't hurt, but, mostly, he wanted his treat. The militia private was formidable, however, so he wandered up to Duke of Gloucester Street to a drink from a horse-watering trough. That is when a stray bulldog decided that the trough belonged to him, and strangers were not welcome. The dog, with its muscular build and combative personality, stood snarling and drooling at Rex, who ignored the show and continued to drink.

Two well-dressed men, Mr. Courtney and Mr. Wells, were walking toward their horses after a night at the Eagle Tavern and witnessed the posturing.

"Ah," said Wells, his eyes twinkling, "the Devil Dog has reappeared to protect his fiefdom, which is, by all accounts, the entire city of Williamsburg."

"I am full of wonder that the beast has not been shot long ago," Courtney said shaking his head.

"He is a wily, tough one," winked Wells. "Some say he will never be caught nor killed despite the best efforts of citizenry and constabulary alike."

"Still, 'tis quite an animal he confronts this evening. I wager the outcome of this impending conflict might well be in doubt."

"Wager, you say?" Wells asked.

"Our next bill at the tavern says the big dog will at last dethrone the bulldog from his perch high above the back-alley mongrel kingdom."

"A wager I accept with pleasure, sir," Wells smiled. "Although the gold dog is a stout animal, I trust the Devil Dog will call upon his history and vicious tenacity to overcome the obvious weight disadvantage."

The two men shook on the bet and backed away a few feet to watch what would happen.

The bulldog was only half Rex's size, but his chest and neck rippled with muscles, and his jaws were massive and vise powerful. In addition, this would not be the alley dog's first fight. He was covered in scars, and his left ear was half gone. The growl deepened, and he took two bowlegged steps toward Rex, whose gold hair went straight up on his back as he turned to greet the thug with a teeth-exposed challenging growl of his own.

Not an animal to wait on the first blow, the bulldog lunged for Rex's throat but missed the kill shot by an inch. Instead of clamping down on the big dog's windpipe, the steel jaws grabbed a mouthful of hair and collar, but he held on. He tried to shake Rex by the collar, but he was dealing with a huge ox-strong animal who not only did not go down but lifted the bulldog's four feet off the ground and slammed him against the heavy wooden trough. Still, the bulldog held on and shook his head and jaws violently. Then Rex's collar broke, and, in a fraction of a second, the bully was on his back, and Rex's jaws were around his neck.

For a brief period, the bulldog flailed, shook, and kicked with his powerful legs, but Rex clamped down with massive force. A few more seconds and the intimidator went limp and emitted a pitiful whimper. Rex shook the animal twice and then released him. The defeated dog lay on his back, submissive.

"Well done!" cheered Wells. "Excellent!"

Rex thoroughly marked the trough area and let the bulldog slink off with its tail between its legs.

"I say, what would this be?" Courtney asked as he leaned down and picked up the ripped collar that still had the bandana pouch attached. "There appears to be some sort of paper in this. Let us step back into the tavern and see what we see in the light."

Holding a bandana containing a document that could change the outcome of the war, Courtney and his friend Wells turned and walked back down the street toward the Eagle. As Wells reached for the door, Rex stuck his nose between the two men, grabbed the collar and pouch with his teeth, and was gone.

"What the bloody . . . !" Courtney exclaimed.

Rex swaggered back toward Lafayette's headquarters. The new alpha dog in town was hungry.

When he got close to the big dwelling, he could smell molasses cakes. It was a warm night, and the aroma came from the open window in General Lafayette's office. Rex put his front paws up on the windowsill and looked in. The door to the hall was closed, and there were no people inside. There was, however, a napkin-covered basket sitting on the general's desk.

An hour later, General Lafayette entered his office, stopped in his tracks, and laughed out loud. Rex lay flat on his back with all four feet up in the air. There was an empty basket off to the side. The laughter woke the dog, but, groggy, he just looked through his legs at Lafayette and yawned.

"*Bonjour!* I trust you've made yourself comfortable in my absence," the general said.

Rex looked comfortable indeed, but he rolled over, stood, and greeted the amused Frenchman.

"What have we here?" he asked and untied the bandana that lay on the floor next to Rex's broken collar.

An hour later, as Lafayette's valet replaced Rex's collar with a portion of a belt, Lafayette and three of his senior officers came to a studied consensus.

"Items one, three, and four are accurate and easy to verify, thus lending *validité* to items two and five," Lafayette said. "We know from the mark, however, that this is not a true document. Therefore, items two and five are *faux*."

"And, if those two items are false, what says that of the British situation?" a major asked.

"Lord Cornwallis is *en péril,* indeed," Lafayette answered and turned over the document.

He drummed his fingers over James's drawing of the flags and ships.

"The French fleet beat the English to the bay, and Cornwallis is trapped."

"Begging the general's pardon," a tough, older colonel said, "but this information was delivered by a dog, and I see its content to be more than open to interpretation if not without merit."

"We might well win this war thanks to this dog, his master, and his friend," Lafayette said in a short tone. "They define *courage*. I know their methods and ingenuity. What they deliver is not to be questioned."

The colonel went stone-faced but said no more.

"We will need to send a dispatch rider to General Washington immediately."

The officers all stood and went about their duties. General Lafayette went to the window, clasped his hands behind his back, and looked out at the patriot troops on the green. Rex rested his head on the sill, and the general rubbed his ears.

"Merci beaucoup," he said to the dog. "But what fate became your master?"

*****

Nate kneeled by Sergeant Adickes's bunk. He held the dagger with both hands and raised it to full arm's length above the snoring man's heart.

Chapter 14

"Attack or escape to fight another day!" Colonel Banastre Tarleton practically yelled at Lord Cornwallis. "Sitting on an arse never battle won!"

The room went as quiet as a tomb. The other officers around the table did not know whether His Lordship would strip Tarleton of his rank, have him hanged, or run him through on the spot.

Tarleton was not popular with the senior officers. There was always a lingering cloud over his victories and escapades; something about the boyish colonel was a little too violent, a tad too primal. He was barely tolerated by the league of gentlemanly generals. Lord Cornwallis himself did not much care for Tarleton, but, like most commanders, he often needed a man who would do the dirty work no one else could or would tackle. Tarleton was his bulldog.

Cornwallis fixed an unblinking stare on the colonel and said with great calm, "You are excused, colonel."

Tarleton returned the look for a few seconds and then turned and stalked from the room.

He vaulted onto his horse and pounded toward the river. Still fuming when he reached the waterfront, Tarleton drew his sword on a fisherman who had just returned to port and was cleaning the long day's debris from the deck of his small craft.

"My horse and I! Across the water now!" he screamed and poked the tip of his weapon against the frightened man's Adam's apple.

It took no time at all for the fisherman to lay off his lines and ferry Tarleton and his huge black horse across the York. There was no payment to the man, but he was just happy to be alive. He had never seen such crazy eyes on a human being.

Tarleton jumped his horse from the small boat and spurred him up the trail toward the dragoon camp. Night or not, he was going to whip up his dragoons and create some havoc in the countryside. He wanted to kill somebody.

So did Nate, but it was not as easy as he had imagined. He had been holding the dagger above the sergeant's heart for over a minute. All he had to do was plunge it down, and his family would be avenged. He closed his eyes and had one last debate in his head. The image of his mother's bruised and broken body flashed through his brain, and he tightened his grip on the dagger.

RAT-A-TAT-TAT! TAT! RAT-A-TAT-TAT! TAT! RAT-A-TAT-TAT! TAT!

An enraged Tarleton had rousted up his fifers and drummers, and they were now trilling and beating out an incessant call to arms. Sergeant Adickes and his tent-mates were still mostly drunk and deeply asleep, but years of responding to the drums overrode their coma-like state and forced open their bloodshot eyes.

"Pox!" "Vile dogs!" and much worse obscenities rang around the tent as the men stumbled and fell all over each other trying to wake up, get up, and straighten up their uniforms.

"And where's my cursed dagger then?!" Adickes shouted, but, before he could look for it, a sword brushed back the tent flap.

"The last man in the saddle loses an ear," Colonel Tarleton said in a frightening tone.

Adickes and the other cavalrymen bolted from the tent and for their horses at a dead run. The animals were saddled in record time, and, within three minutes of the drum call, the entire unit was galloping after Colonel Tarleton through the midnight woods. The last man in line had blood streaming down the side of his face from where most of his left ear used to be.

"Lord," Nate prayed, "I thank thee for making it a warm night."

Had it been cold, the soldiers' blankets would not have been strewn about the floor where Nate could easily duck under one and lie still in the darkness.

Nate did not move until he was sure the dragoons were really gone. After a few minutes, he peeked out of the tent flap and saw that the dragoon area of the camp was empty and there were no visible sentries. Staying in the shadows of the trees, he crept down to the river's edge where he leaned against a dilapidated old dock and hoped for someone to sail by. It was a clear, starry night, and the boy spent some time looking up at the heavens and trying to decide if Tarleton's drummers had saved the sergeant's life or his own soul.

A few minutes after dawn, an awkward boat with a square sail transporting dozens of pigs and their grizzled owner plowed along near the shoreline.

"Ahoy! Ahoy there!" Nate yelled. "I shall be greatly obliged to you, sir, for a ride across the river!"

The man had his hands full with the ill-handling craft and seemed out of sorts in general.

"If it's a ferry'n you be needin', you've hailed the wrong conveyance," he shouted back. "My commerce is on this side."

"A guinea for your trouble!" yelled Nate and held up his payment from RummyJim.

"'Tis a fine morning for a leisurely sail across the lovely York River," the man said, his mood completely changed by the coin. "She's a cantankerous old tub, but she'll deliver you safe and sound. Wade out here, and I'll hoist you aboard!"

"Wade? It's too deep!"

"Once I get'r goin', 'tis a faulty choice to beach her."

Nate thought that he must be somehow destined to flail around in the water for all time.

"Here I come," he shouted.

He splashed into the water, which came up to his neck before he reached the boat. The man made him hand up the coin before pulling him onto the boat and then rushing back to the tiller and sail. It was such an unwieldy craft that, without constant attention, it would bog and founder. Nate had to wedge himself between the pigs that were packed onto the small deck. It was a snorting, smelly ride across the river to Yorktown.

*****

James's walk back to Yorktown had been equally uncomfortable. His punctured foot was swollen, and the pain was intense. A mile from the British camp, he knew he could not go much further.

Over the past few weeks, James and Miriam, the towering cook at Cornwallis's headquarters, had become friends. They enjoyed each other's intelligence and bantering style. During conversations in the kitchen, he learned that she had once been a slave but had aligned herself with the British and their promise of freedom as the redcoats marched past the plantation where she had spent her entire life. It was a tumultuous time in Miriam's life as her master had died from a fever two weeks before. The man had been only a shade over five feet tall, and, when seen interacting with his very tall, longtime cook, the effect was comical.

"All I could see talkin' to the man was the top of his little bald head," Miriam had laughed.

"How'd you end up wit Lord Cornwallis?" James asked one afternoon as he waited for Miriam to finish preparing some mutton.

"Massa Duncan died. Now, he wa'n't no angel, but he treated me pretty good. Well, it turn out he left me to his sister, who 'bout the most disagreeable woman I ever seen. Mean as a snake. 'Bout that time, them redcoats come a'marchin' in here, and I figured I'd move on over to that side. Couldn't be no worse'n bein' beat half to death by that woman."

She lifted the mutton from a table and placed it on a platter by James.

"And I'm free."

James knew he was close to where Miriam had told him she lived.

"Massa Duncan wa'n't hardly cold in the ground, and I been gone 'bout a week, when I heared his evil sister shut down the old place, taked all Massa's money, and bought herself a fine house up Philadelphia way," Miriam had said as they walked across the rear yard early one morning. "Well, when I heared dat, I jest up and moved right back in the little house that been the only place I ever lived in."

"The slave quarters?" James asked.

"Home," she replied.

James dragged toward a weak light flickering in the distance.

"Lord! What got hold of yo foot?!" Miriam exclaimed as she helped James into her tiny, dirt-floored house. "A wolf?!"

The small, rough-hewn wood cabin was about the size of James's quarters back on the Armistead plantation, but this space was more personal. There were two dolls with clay-baked heads and straw-filled bodies on a narrow shelf.

"You got a daughter?" James asked in a kind, interested way.

"Not no more," Miriam said and looked away. James let it go.

An African bead necklace, Miriam's only link to her ancestry, hung on the wall. Her late husband's shoes sat polished next to the tiny stone fireplace. Her narrow bed was covered in a colorful hand-woven blanket. A wispy homespun curtain dyed orange with the roots of the madder plant covered the only small window. Some stew bubbled in an iron pot hanging over the fire.

"Well, I was walkin' to . . ."

"And what yo sorry carcass a'doin' wanderin' 'round in the middle of the night to begin wit?"

"The truth is . . ."

"You wouldn't know no truth if it come a'ridin' up on a blue horse a'blowin' a French horn! Prop that big ugly foot up chere," Miriam ordered. "Sit down. Lord! If you a'n't gettin' in some kind'a mess one place, you stirrin' up sumpin' somewhere else."

"I . . . yes, Miriam."

Within an hour, Miriam had cooked up a root-based paste and pressed it to James's injured foot with a linen-strip bandage.

"I was wonderin' 'bout them British and makin' slaves free and all," James said with some skepticism.

"I'm listenin.'"

"Supposin' General Washington come a'gallopin' up to His Lordship wavin' a white flag and give up tomorrow. I jest wonder what'd become'a us then."

"We could go on down the road or whatever else we had a mind to do. The British gents'd take care of us."

"Well, so they say."

In the morning, Miriam headed back to Yorktown to fire up the ovens at Cornwallis's headquarters. Her movement woke James, and his first thought was to wonder if Rex had made it and, if so, had Lafayette been able to figure out his marks and drawing. He thought he would make his way to his job and assure Tompkins that Lafayette had accepted the fake document whether he had or not. The poultice the cook had applied to his foot was working, and the pain was tolerable, but he would be walking slowly for a while.

*****

On the Yorktown docks, Nate was running for his life. RummyJim had spotted him when he exited the pig boat.

The sutler's face went crimson as he screamed, "Thief!"

Nate hightailed it.

"Stop the lad!" RummyJim roared. "He's a boat-stealin', rum-thievin' pirate!"

Luckily, no one paid much attention to RummyJim's frequent outbursts, so there was no groundswell among the citizenry to intercept the fleeing boy. The rum merchant, however, was boiling mad and swinging a hefty walking stick as he huffed and puffed after the fleet-footed Nate. The chase wound through piles of cargo and equipment on the dock, past the supply wagons along the waterfront, and down an alley by the few residences at shore level. A dead end! Nate was backed up against a shoring wall and boxed in by the rear of a house on one side and a vertical slope on the other.

"Where . . . is . . . my . . . boat?!" RummyJim gasped pointing the stick at Nate.

"Why, that fine craft is at the bottom of the York River, sir," Nate said in a completely calm voice.

"Arrrrgh!" RummyJim's face was so red it looked like it was going to explode at any second. "My (gasp, pant) rum?!"

"Hmm, I believe that is presently in the bellies of His Majesty's dragoons."

The boy seemed to be totally at ease and unconcerned about the livid dealer and his stick.

"Yah! And my guinea?!"

"Ah, now that went to a good-hearted pig farmer."

"I'll peel you like an onion, dip you in salt, and leave you floppin' on the shore like a flounder!"

"And justified you would be, sir."

"Grr," RummyJim growled.

He took a step toward Nate and raised the cane.

“Of course, if you peel, dip, and leave me flopping, I don’t see how you’ll take ownership of the fifty hogsheads of fine brandy.”

“Eh?” RummyJim narrowed his eyes. “Brandy?”

“Surely you’ve heard tale of my Uncle Micah and his distillery. There’s those who say a brace of generals on both sides won’t set foot in or out of battle lest they have a dollop of Micah Chandler’s brandy.”

“I, uh . . . how does that save your worthless, lyin’, thievin’ hide?”

“My uncle is in Richmond, and the fifty hogsheads sit unguarded though their precise location is quite secret to all but family.”

RummyJim rubbed his chin.

“Fifty, you say.”

“True. Undoubtedly sad compensation for your fine vessel and wares, yet . . .”

“Show me.”

RummyJim pulled a pistol from his belt. Holding the weapon in Nate’s back, he pushed the boy through the bustle and up the hill. As they walked past the Nelson house, the boy saw James walking toward the back gate. At least a dozen armed soldiers were in the yard patrolling the headquarters.

“Ah, excellent timing!” Nate said excitedly indicating James. “He has a key we’ll require to get the brandy.”

“What’s that? Stop! One pinch of trickery and . . .”

Nate walked away from the pistol in his back, weaved between the guards, and over to the wall gate before RummyJim could react. He wanted to shoot, but there were way too many soldiers around, and, besides, there were fifty hogsheads of brandy in the mix.

"Wondered where you been a'hidin'," James said under his breath as he reached the wall.

"Diverting the man in the purple greatcoat would serve me a great purpose," Nate whispered.

Without hesitation, James cried out to the house guards, "That's the man! That scoundrel in the purple coat and red boots! He the sorry sort who stole His Lordship's apple pie from Miriam's kitchen sill! Git that man!"

"Apple pie?" RummyJim said. "What . . ."

The bored guards cut their eyes over to a confused RummyJim.

"Yes, sir, His Lordship'll keep a good eye on the man who brings to task the pie-stealin' man!"

The guards charged.

"There you go, boys! His Lordship like nothin' more than his apple pie! Drag that sorry pie-thievin' scoundrel by the kitchen, and let Miriam baste his sorry head wit a heavy spoon fore you put'm in irons!"

Four of the burly soldiers grabbed the loudly cursing RummyJim and carried him away.

Nate whispered, "Does Lafayette know of the French ships?"

James nodded.

Nate turned to leave and then looked back with sadness in his eyes.

"Rex . . . he . . . he . . . drowned," he said with a tremor in his voice.

"Rex is fit as a fiddle," James whispered. "About now, he's probly dinin' on a fine piece'a beef with General Lafayette."

Nate's eyes lit up, and he struck his right fist into his left palm with glee.

"Wonderful! Thank the Lord!" he said as quietly as he could. "I must go. My thanks, my friend."

With that, he ran down to the street and kept going until he reached the spot a half mile away where he had tied Milk. Although he was tempted to heel the big horse into a gallop, he rode at a leisurely and unsuspicious pace through the camp and onto the Williamsburg road. He passed through the familiar sentries with a nod and a smile.

Nate knew his spying days at the Yorktown British camp were over. Once RummyJim talked his way out of the pie-stealing rap, the spirit dealer would smear his name with every camp follower, soldier, and officer within earshot. Being branded a thief would be bad enough, but it would be just a matter of time before someone figured out what he was really doing.

Henry gave James a freshly laundered shirt and brushed off his coat before he would allow him to report to Tompkins.

"And you a'n't goin' nowhere in this house witout shoes," the old slave ordered. "And you'll take in tea for His Lordship."

Tompkins sat at a table with several other officers including General O'Hara. Cornwallis was at the head of the table intently studying a map. Even though his wounded foot throbbed in the shoe, James expertly served tea to the men and then quietly took his place against the wall.

"Admiral Graves will be engaging de Grasse in a matter of hours," Cornwallis said.

There was a great, collective sigh of relief around the table.

"With nineteen ships," His Lordship added.

The relief was short-lived.

"Nineteen?!" O'Hara exclaimed. "There are twenty-eight French frigates and cruisers bristling with cannons breathing down our necks! Sir Rodney has triple that number at his disposal!"

"Sir Rodney has taken ill and returned to England with his fleet," Cornwallis informed them. "Admirals Hood and Graves have been left nineteen ships, and that is the number they will use to either defeat the French or transport our army back north."

"Pardon my insolence, sir," a general said, "but that would appear to be a tentative outcome at best."

"And Lafayette . . ." , said another.

"The Royal Navy will win the sea," Cornwallis said with finality. "And I will not suffer defeat at the hands of a French boy."

The meeting was over. Except for Tompkins, all of the officers rose with Cornwallis and exited. The captain questioned James and was pleased that the fake document had been delivered, but his mind was racing with a far greater concern. Like everyone else who had been in the room, he felt a net tightening and did not know what to do about it.

"What instruction did you receive from Lafayette?" he asked.

"Jest to keep my eyes and ears open and to keep on a'bringin' whatever I see and hear."

"Good. There will be another missive to deliver on the morrow."

James left the meeting thinking war was a complex thing. Mr. Armistead had been right: once you beat the other man in his head, the guns and bayonets fall quickly. He did not know if the British were at that point, but he could sure see one thing—the French ships and Washington's main army marching south were eating at them.

*****

The second reunion between Nate and Rex was as lively as the first.

"He wanted to go back," Lafayette said, "but I had a sense you would make an appearance soon and used all manner of shameless bribery to keep him with me."

"I suspect the cakes may have entered the persuasion," Nate laughed as he pitched yet another treat to his dog.

"*Son appétit* is not in question," the general smiled. "Now, what do we make of you? I agree that your usefulness at the camp has run its course. We owe you *une dette d'honneur*."

"I did little, but thank you, sir."

"You've earned my compliance with your personal ambition. What next would you most like to do?"

Without hesitation, Nate said, "Fight."

The young general looked at him for a few seconds and then nodded.

As Nate turned to leave, he hesitated and said, "One thing more, general, if I may speak, sir."

"Proceed," Lafayette prompted.

"In the course of my actions, I stole a sutler's boat, which shortly thereafter sunk, and its cargo is gone. There is not much noble about the man, but, still, I feel guilt at his loss at my hand." Nate looked Lafayette in the eye and continued, "It weighs on me, sir."

"When the more pressing business of this conflict is resolved," Lafayette assured him, "this man will be compensated if from my personal funds."

"I thank you, sir," Nate responded and left the room.

Sergeant Harrington got Nate outfitted with one of the few new uniforms available in the entire camp, a sword, and a musket. Nate was embarrassed by the clean, fresh uniform as so many of the veteran soldiers wore tattered, stained, and frayed gear. There were other fresh recruits dressed in new uniforms, and some of the old hands had a fresh piece here or there, but, still, the boy felt uncomfortable about the situation.

"Oh, ye'll be a nasty, scruffy lad in no time," Harrington laughed. "Just wait until you've dug a trench or two."

The big veteran soldier had a personal liking for the boy and gave him individual instruction with the weapons in addition to the endless drills on the green.

"You've got as keen a natural eye for the musket as anyone I've trained," the sergeant said. "And 'tis a gift to come in handy against the British. They're a stodgy lot, but the lads can fight."

"When?" Nate asked.

"Soon."

*****

The British navy officer could not have looked more hangdog if he tried, but he was not putting on a show. The news he had to deliver to Lord Cornwallis was depressing enough to put even the most optimistic of officers into a dark mood. He dreaded the confrontation but stood up straight and followed James into Cornwallis's private office. To his surprise, other than the slave, who stood unobtrusively against a far wall, His Lordship was alone in the room.

"Your report, if you please, colonel," the nobleman said in an unexpectedly kind tone.

The colonel cleared his throat and said, "The sea battle off the Capes was indecisive, sir."

"Perhaps more detail would paint me a clearer picture," Cornwallis suggested.

On September 5, the British fleet of nineteen ships under the command of Admiral Graves appeared off the Virginia Capes. The French ships under de Grasse were already at anchor in the bay and outnumbered the British ships two to one. The fleets fought an indecisive battle known as the battle of the Capes that lasted only two hours. About equal damage was done to both sides.

"The maneuvers were well executed by both sides, but the shear number of French vessels was clear to eventually gain a decisive advantage," the colonel said.

"How stand the naval operations presently?"

"I . . . I loathe to report, sir, that Admiral Graves has turned his fleet north and is en route back to New York."

Cornwallis absorbed the information and sat still and silent for almost a full minute. After that interminable pause, he looked at the nervous officer.

"Thank you, colonel," he said calmly. "That is all."

The man gratefully exited the room.

"A glass of port, please, James," Cornwallis said softly.

Without a word, the slave brought the worried man his drink. His Lordship sipped it slowly. Another minute of silence passed during which Cornwallis closed his eyes and did not move a muscle. Then he rubbed the back of his neck and spoke to James.

"Take one of my horses and ride to Lafayette. Tell him you overheard me say four British transports sneaked through the French armada. Those four transports contain five thousand troops, three thousand cannonballs, and two hundred cannons."

"Yes, sir, I'll do that very thing. 'Course I a'n't seen no four transports, but that won't be the first thing I a'n't seen neither."

"There are no transports," His Lordship said as he rubbed his eyes, "but the longer I can delay a siege, the more time the navy has to come back and get us out of here."

"You think they'll come back?" James asked.

"They must," Cornwallis said in a weak voice. "They must."

Chapter 15

It was late afternoon when Nate and the other recruits were finally dismissed after a full day of drills and loading and reloading practice with their muskets. Some of the other soldiers complained about the training.

"Dandy lot of good all this marching around in circles does a man," one of them griped. "I got me musket and sword. All I need now is a lobsterback on the other end of either."

Fighting in the Revolutionary War was basically a toe-to-toe shoot-out. The key to victory was to get in a good first volley, take a return fire, and then reload faster than the enemy. The option in close quarters was man-to-man combat with fixed bayonets. Therefore, most of the training dealt with loading and firing drills, over and over until the motions were mechanical. Loading and firing the musket were done in thirteen counts:

1. Half-cock firelock.
2. Handle cartridge. (Bite off top and cover with thumb.)
3. Prime. (Shake powder into pan.)
4. Shut pan.
5. Charge with cartridge.
6. Draw ramrod.
7. Ram down cartridge.

8. Return ramrod.
9. Shoulder weapon.
10. Poise weapon.
11. Cock firelock.
12. Take aim.
13. Fire!

Once a new recruit could handle his musket smoothly, he was placed in a group of three, then a group of twelve. They were taught to wheel and dress to the right and left. Alignment and dressing the ranks was practiced constantly, but not for show. Straight, orderly lines made for a smooth and effective firing sequence.

Nate did not complain, but he was in some agreement with the ones who did. He did not really see the point in the constant marching back and forth, perfecting the turns, and instant compliance to the dozens of spoken or drumbeat orders that seemed so important to the training officers. Comfortable with Sergeant Harrington, he asked him about it as the two walked across the green toward supper.

"Wherin lies the value in all the marching, sir?"

"A question often contemplated and easily answered," he replied. "What do you do when I order 'About-face'?"

"I turn to the right and face the opposite direction."

"Without thinking?"

"No thought, sir. Not after doing it a hundred or more times."

"When an officer raises his sword, and the drums beat out the signal to charge, you'll do so. Without thought," Harrington added. "And the firing and reloading of your musket will be instinctive, automatic."

Thinking, Nate walked a few steps and then said, "So, it is about following orders."

"Blindly. And repetition. Otherwise, there is no army. 'Tis but an unwieldy group of men thrashing about with muskets and swords."

Nate nodded, and they walked on to the cooking tents. The boy stood in line with the other soldiers. He looked across the camp area and saw a familiar sight.

"A good thing James is an excellent spy," he laughed to himself. "He certainly has no future as a cavalryman."

One of Lord Cornwallis's fine horses was trotting along the street. Barely hanging onto the saddle, James was trying to guide the animal through traffic and up to Lafayette's headquarters.

"I can't stop this demon!" he yelled at a young private in the yard.

The soldier laughed, held up a hand, and said firmly, "Whoa."

The horse stopped immediately, and the man took the animal's bridle.

"Fine looking steed," he said.

"He's the devil!" James said as he awkwardly dismounted and walked toward the front steps.

Lafayette and his staff were gathered in the general's office when James was shown into the chamber. Lafayette ended a report and turned to his spy.

"You have news?"

"Yes, sir, I do," James said respectfully. "Not a whole lot in the way of true battle happen out on the bay, but the British ships turned back for New York."

The officers around the table cut each other gleeful looks. This was the best news they could have heard.

"You are sure of this information?" Lafayette asked.

"Yes indeed, general, sir. I was a standin' right there in the room when the officer give the report to Lord Cornwallis hisself."

The officers seemed near bursting into cheers, but they waited for Lafayette to set the tone.

"Anything else?"

"Well, sir, His Lordship tell me to tell you that four British ships got through somehow or other and they's just full'a men and cannons and such."

"Did they?"

"No, sir, there a'n't no four ships."

Unable to restrain himself, one of the officers shouted, "Huzzah! We've trapped them!"

Others joined in.

Lafayette slapped his hand down on the table, and the celebration ended.

"We are part of *une force majeure,*" he said. "As military men, we will never see such *une gêne de richesses* again. The only barriers in our way are arrogance, overconfidence, and premature *célébration*. Until Lord Cornwallis surrenders his sword to General Washington, we will embody *l'esprit de noblesse* and prepare our men."

The officers all looked sheepish and went quiet.

"What is General Washington's progress?"

"Generals Washington, Rochambeau, and their parties will arrive in a matter of days," a general said. "And their fourteen thousand troops a fortnight later."

"*Merci*. Dismissed," General Lafayette said.

James was going to exit with the officers, but Lafayette signaled him to stay. He stood sternly by while James shut the door behind the men.

A few seconds of silence and then the Frenchman threw his arms straight up into the air, lit up with a wide smile, and exclaimed, "*Voilà! La victoire* is near!"

*****

In decades past, the citizens of Williamsburg anticipated the arrival of a new royal governor with great excitement. The pomp and circumstance surrounding such an event lent a festive air to the city. People welcomed the new governor and, sometimes, his family to his palace in the city with much cheering and generally open arms.

No past arrival had come close to generating the kind of excitement the anticipation of General George Washington did. He was the symbol of the revolution, and his coming physical presence was like an injection of hope, a sign that the dream was real.

As with everything else in the army, rumors swirled around Washington's coming. Some said he would appear in a grand carriage. Others had heard he would ride in alone. Some regulars at the taverns claimed to know he was already in town but in disguise. No one knew for sure when he would arrive in Williamsburg as the trip from Mount Vernon was over roads that often flooded out, the general might have important stops to make along the way, horses get tired, and other factors hung over every trip made in colonial Virginia. Lafayette did post a mounted lookout on the road who, upon sighting Washington, was to gallop back to camp with the news.

On September 14, the news was good.

"Everyone on your feet!" Sergeant Harrington ordered as he moved quickly through the relaxing soldiers.

"Up straight, men! Button up. Look your best! General Washington is only a mile away!"

The troops jumped up, grabbed their tunics and other uniform pieces, and streamed out onto the green.

"We'll actually get to see him!" another private said to Nate as they frantically tried to get fastened up.

"They say he is as tall as a tree," Nate said and, with the others, fell into formation.

The officers rushed back and forth trying to put together a proper line of soldiers to greet Washington, Rochambeau, and other officers.

General Lafayette enthusiastically greeted his friend Washington with an embrace. He also embraced his fellow French officers, and then the officers began a walk along the lines, reviewing the troops.

When they were only a few men away from Nate, Rex appeared and sat down in front of his master. Sergeant Harrington shot a look their way.

"Rex, go. Go away," Nate whispered down at his dog.

But Rex saw Lafayette coming. Maybe there was a treat in this for him. Everyone was at attention, and Nate did not know what to do. The generals reached him, but Rex remained planted right at his feet. Nate was sure his military career was over.

"And this young *guerrier* and his dog have provided invaluable assistance to me in many ways," Lafayette said in a sincere voice.

"Excellent," Washington responded. "It is the young warriors who make those of us with generals' epaulets look competent. And what a fine dog! He reminds me somewhat of my own favorite, a devilish companion named Vulcan."

General Washington leaned down and rubbed Rex's ears, and then the awe-inspiring generals moved on down the line.

The patriot soldiers were impressed that the great Washington had spoken to Nate, but the fact that he had actually rubbed Rex's head turned the dog into a bona fide good-luck-charm celebrity. Over the next few days, soldier after soldier dropped by to touch the head touched by George Washington for luck.

The next morning, Lafayette said to James, "I need you to go back. We are at a most critical stage, and every piece of information is of *la plus haute importance*."

"Well, sir, I got the 'importance' part. I'll go back witout no quarrel," James said, "but I'll miss stridin' 'round in this fine new uniform."

"It will be brought to Yorktown," the general assured him. "When the time is right, I shall *je serai fier* for you to wear it at my side."

"That's mighty gracious, general. Well, I guess I'll change clothes and get back up on Satan fo the ride back."

"Lord Cornwallis's horse is named Satan?" Lafayette asked, surprised.

"Well, general, if it a'n't, it oughta be," James quipped.

More and more Continental troops, both American and French, filtered into Williamsburg over the next two weeks. But, what turned Williamsburg from a town with a military presence into a bursting-at-the-seams staging area for war was the arrival of General Washington's main force of fourteen thousand men on September 26.

Nate's concerns about his shiny new uniform faded quickly when the French troops marched into town.

By comparison, Nate looked like a scavenger in rags. The French uniforms were brilliantly white, and each regiment wore its own color on collars and lapels. The sergeants sported ostrich plumes in their caps, and the duke of Lauzun's officers had tiger-skin saddlecloths on their horses.

Nate was now one of seventeen thousand American and French soldiers eager for the battle to begin. It soon did. Even though it was twelve miles to Yorktown, the forces left at five in the morning on September 28 and, by dark, were within one mile of the eight thousand soldiers in the British camp.

A veteran of the trip, Rex spent a good bit of time out in front of the long column sniffing around. Periodically, he would run back to where Nate was marching with his unit. As he moved among the soldiers, he received many pats and rubs from the men who had adopted the dog as unofficial mascot.

"I tell ye, true," a private of Irish descent said to his marching mates, "a dog may be just a dog, but me heart sings a different tune of this animal. He's a good luck charm, he is. Like our own glorious little leprechaun to ward off the dangers of battle, he is."

Transporting and positioning the artillery took a few more days, but, on October 9, the bombardment began. It was one relentless blast after another. A continual blaze of shot and shell whistled overhead, straight for the British fortifications.

When the first round of cannon blasts shook the earth, Rex dropped flat to the ground and did not move a muscle. If he could have covered his ears, he would have.

Sergeant Harrington was nearby and said, "Ah! So a war dog you want to be is it? Then up with you, boy! Soon, the noise will be no more alarming than a roll of distant thunder. Up now!"

The big dog stood up just as another barrage screamed over their heads. This time, Rex got mad and started barking loudly at the cannon blasts. Sergeant Harrington and the others laughed.

"That's the lad!" Harrington said.

Within an hour, Rex did not even flinch no matter how many cannons were firing.

The men also somehow got used to the booming artillery and carried on as if the incredible racket was just a minor background annoyance. Along with most of the patriot soldiers, Nate dug trenches for days. He did not mind the work since he knew the ditches would advance the army and save soldiers from the field cannons. After a long shift in the trench, Nate was walking back from a water pail when he spotted his friend from the Green Spring battle. As usual, Isaac was in high spirits as he helped some other men position a cannon.

"Greetings, my friend!" Isaac shouted when he saw Nate.

"So, you are an artillery man now," Nate grinned as he clasped Isaac's hand.

"Indeed I am!" Isaac replied. "Why, in an hour's time or so, this very weapon will leave a mark not soon forgotten by the redcoat scoundrels!"

"How far will it shoot?" Nate asked.

"Nearly a mile, she will," Isaac answered. "And, before it all settles, we'll have nigh to four hundred artillery pieces aimed right down the British gullet."

"Four hundred!" Nate exclaimed. "What a noise that will be when they all fire at once!"

"No, no," Isaac laughed. "Not all at once. We rotate these lovely weapons. Need to give them a chance to cool down so that they don't cook off."

"Cook off?" Nate was puzzled.

"Ignite the powder while we're loading it," Isaac explained. "Back to work for me, my boy! Good luck to you in the coming conflict!"

Nate returned the good wishes and went back to digging. He held up his end of the task, but there was something else in the wind, and the boy wanted to be a part of it.

"Begging the colonel's pardon," he said as Colonel Alexander Hamilton finally exited his tent in the late afternoon and walked alone toward his horse.

"Yes?" Hamilton responded.

"My name is Nate Chandler, sir. The redcoats almost killed my parents and destroyed our farm."

"My sympathies, young sir. There have been many tragedies in the course of our conflict."

"I would consider it an honor to volunteer for your charge on the redoubt, sir."

"For revenge?"

"For truth, partly so, but I also feel battle is where I can most be of consequence."

"Boldly spoken, but my new aide, a Sergeant Harrington, has selected the four hundred who will execute the attack. I rely on his judgment."

"As do I, sir."

*****

BOOM! The first shell hit the ground by Miriam's kitchen at the Nelson house. The impact shattered the south brick wall of the outbuilding and sent the cook and her helpers running through the rubble for cover. BAM! CRASH! The second mortar round blasted through part of the roof and crushed a chimney. BOOM! BAM! CRASH! Cannonball number three was a direct hit on the room next to Lord Cornwallis's office, where His Lordship was working alone. James was serving him afternoon tea.

The blast threw both men to the floor. Cornwallis hit his head on the corner of his desk and was dazed. BOOM! Another mortar crashed into the house. Stumbling through the debris and smoke, James reached the fallen commander.

"We mus' git out'a here!" he yelled.

He kneeled by Cornwallis and managed to get the older man's arm around his shoulders.

"Come on, Yo Lordship, we movin' now!"

James stood, pulling up the wounded man. Holding the arm around his shoulders and with his own arm around Cornwallis's waist, the slave half dragged the commander of the British forces across the crumbling room, through a gaping hole in the wall, and outside.

They lurched across the smoky rear yard and on past the destroyed kitchen toward an arbor at the rear of the property. BANG! BAM! A shell blew apart the dovecote and a heavy gate. James practically carried Cornwallis to an arbor that backed up to a stout wall. The slave lowered the general to the ground by the brick barrier and then sat down beside him.

Cornwallis, still somewhat dazed, looked at James.

"Don't you concern yourself, Yo Lordship," James said. "Couple'a old boys like us is too tough to kill wit a little cannonball."

James was almost positive he saw a trace of a smile on the dour leader's face before several officers rushed up.

"We have a carriage!" one of the officers yelled. "We'll take you to a safe grotto down by the water!"

He and a young lieutenant got on either side of Cornwallis and began walking him around the house.

"Halt!"

Cornwallis was back in control. The officers stopped in their tracks, and Cornwallis pointed back at James.

"He rides in the carriage with me."

*****

Sergeant Harrington was glad to have Nate in the attack unit, but he was also acutely aware of the danger.

"'Tis no drill this," he said, and his eyes were hard. "Charging a redoubt is as dangerous an undertaking as you're liable to participate."

"Why is that?" Nate asked.

Harrington started to continue, but the drums beat out muster, the call to assemble.

"It's time, my lad. You'll know soon enough."

The four hundred men assembled in a trench three hundred yards from Redoubt No. 10. Then they waited for the miners and sappers to do their work. Those men certainly had one of the worst jobs in the world. They went out unarmed in front of the troops to clear a way through the obstructions the enemy had laid before them—sharpened stakes and tangled trunks of trees that helped protect the enemy's position. It was a job so dangerous that these advance teams were known as the "forlorn hope," in reference to their chances of returning alive. It was slow work, and, as the anticipation and fear built in the waiting soldiers, some of the ones who had never been in combat became physically ill.

Rex's presence helped as the huge dog walked among the crouched and nerve-frayed troops.

"There's luck meandering in our presence," the Irishman claimed. "Touch the magic and it'll protect you sure as a shield."

He patted Rex, and every patriot soldier followed suit. It made no logical sense, but the men felt calmer after contact with the good luck dog.

At around seven that night, four hundred French troops crept toward Redoubt No. 9 and a like number of Americans inched their way toward Redoubt No. 10. It was dark, too quiet, and Nate, like every other man in the field, was terrified and running on adrenalin. The boy thought surely the enemy could hear his heart pounding in his chest. Closer. There was no movement from the redoubt or any sign that they had been seen.

A British lookout on Redoubt No. 10 heard something and spotted the invaders. Musket fire flashed from the redoubt. The miners and sappers yelled that an opening was cut.

"Charge, my boys! Charge, charge!" Colonel Hamilton shouted. "Bayonets! Bayonets!"

Waving his sword, Hamilton led the way through the opening in the debris and up the dirt-packed wall of the redoubt fortress. Climbing over the sharpened stakes halfway up, Hamilton never faded from the lead position. Private Nate Chandler was the second man over the top of the wall. His dog was right on his heels.

Chapter 16

Before Nate joined the army, he would not have been able to guess what being in battle was really like. Now, he knew, but he still could not have described the experience. From the time he started up the redoubt wall until the fighting ended, it was all just a haze of smoke and screams and clanging weapons.

As the boy followed Colonel Hamilton over the top of the redoubt, he yelled and thrust his bayonet the way he had been trained to do, but the action was automatic. He had no conception of doing anything the right or wrong way. The training helped him look past the panic and identify someone on his way to do him harm. He thrust and parried and swung with his musket, fists, and feet. He kicked one man to the ground, bit another who grabbed him from behind, crashed his musket stock into a redcoat knee. Like every other soldier in the fight, he wrestled, punched, stabbed, and slashed in a fierce, primal effort to stay alive.

A wounded British soldier on his knees behind Nate clawed around for his musket on the ground and then lurched forward to drive the weapon's bayonet into the small of the boy's back. He never got there. Rex exploded out of the foggy madness like a ghost and crushed the attacker's throat in his jaws.

The smoke and the din did not have much effect

on Rex. His remarkable canine nose knew the familiar scents of the patriots and the new, intrusive smell of the men who were hurting members of his pack. The powerful dog attacked the men in red coats over and over. He charged and bit and shook and overpowered.

"Up the berm, lads!" Sergeant Harrington shouted as the British started to retreat. "Run the scoundrels back to England!"

The British soldiers were outnumbered, and the patriots' ferocious fighting sent the redcoats crawling madly up the far side of the trench. The patriots charged up after them, but most of the enemy got over the top and ran for their lives across a field.

Then it was over.

"Stand down!" shouted Colonel Hamilton from on top of the berm. "Huzzah, boys! We whipped them good and proper!"

Victory yells from the direction of Redoubt No. 9 confirmed that the French assault on that target had been successful as well.

A cheer went up from the veteran soldiers, but most of the rookies, like Nate, just shook and took breath after grateful breath. Rex found his master and stood by his side. The dog's muzzle, neck, and chest were drenched in blood not his own.

"Look lively!" Harrington ordered after the brief celebration. "Guard detail, secure the prisoners! Medical officers, tend to the wounded of both sides! Perimeter detail, assume positions! Dispatch, report to General Lafayette!"

The soldiers, flushed with victory, hustled to their assigned duties. Several took a slight detour over to Rex.

"Saved me life, truly," said one as he rubbed the dog's head.

"The cur who had me on the ground will make no more use of his dagger arm," another said and gave Rex a pat. "I never heard such a crack as when his jaws clamped in on the man."

Others had similar praise for the dog, and his status as good luck charm was secure.

*****

With the siege under way, British command was making do with wet walls, dirt floors, and ammunition crates for desks and chairs at headquarters down by the riverfront. The space was nothing more than a cave, referred to as a "grotto," carved into the base of the cliff by centuries of winds and storms.

A tent against the opening of the grotto served as the office anteroom. Inside the cliff, there were two spaces, one for clerical staff and another curtained-off area for Cornwallis's private office. The grotto was so cramped that all of Cornwallis's servants, except James, had been dismissed.

Aides had managed to furnish Cornwallis's office with a proper desk and leather chair. A civilized man, Cornwallis had no intention of missing his evening tea and sweets no matter what was going on in the trenches. James served just as General O'Hara parted the curtain.

"Begging your pardon, sir, but we have news of a most alarming nature."

Cornwallis was not pleased with the intrusion, but he indicated that the general could enter.

"Well?"

"Redoubts 9 and 10 have fallen, sir," he reported.

The British commander exhaled in a slow, measured way but said nothing.

O'Hara cleared his throat and continued, "Those positions will give the enemy cannon a direct, unobstructed field of fire."

Cornwallis still remained silent.

"Ahem. Without the promised men, ships, and armament from New York," O'Hara pointed out what Cornwallis already knew, "our position might well be indefensible in less than four days. We have only slightly more than one hundred mortar rounds and as sad a condition applies to most other provisions."

After studying a map, Cornwallis looked up at O'Hara and said, "I shall ponder this without distraction. Call a general staff meeting for the morning."

"Very good, sir," the general replied and backed from the room.

*****

Nate and his unit spent the rest of the night helping the diggers extend the patriot trenches, incorporating the captured redoubts into the network. It was backbreaking work, but, fresh from victory, the soldiers told high-spirited battle tales as they dug. Some of them spun around Rex.

"I certainly don't mean to imply the dog is otherworldly, you understand," a lanky twenty-year-old corporal said, "and I abhor any reference that might be construed as blasphemous, but I saw what I saw. This fine golden animal sprang to the top of a man's head, pushed away floating like an angel, and then swooped down in an avenging arc severing the head of redcoat after redcoat with his mighty jaws as he whistled by."

"Ah, 'tis no doubt," added a pudgy private. "Why, as I looked through disbelieving eyes, this very same dog grabbed two burly lobsterbacks by the ankles at the same time and, with but a flip of his powerful head, threw both the bloody scoundrels up over the berm where they landed high in a tree."

It went on like that. Nate just smiled and did not try to dispute any of the stories. It was all good fun, and he remembered what Sergeant Harrington had said about an army needing heroes. If his dog was to fill that bill, he saw no harm. At least, he thought, Rex probably wouldn't let it all go to his head and become arrogant as an English dandy.

Just before dawn, they heard musket fire and other sounds of battle coming from a short distance away. They climbed up and saw British infantrymen attacking a patriot artillery unit near a parallel trench less than a hundred yards away. Sergeant Harrington had accompanied Colonel Hamilton back to Lafayette's camp, and the lanky corporal was temporarily in command.

"Charge!" the corporal shouted. "They're attacking our boys! We'll give them a breakfast to remember! Charge!"

Nate and the others poured up out of the trench and ran across the open field. The lanky corporal could run like a deer and was twenty yards ahead of the others. As he approached the battle, the dawn sun came up over the horizon, and he could see most of the attackers perfectly silhouetted against the morning sky. He slid to a stop, spun around, and held up his sword.

"Halt!" he hollered. "Halt!"

Nate and the others stopped running.

"Kneeling! Load, cock, and fire at will!"

Within a few seconds, over three hundred patriot muskets fired at the dark targets so perfectly outlined against a light sky. Dozens of the enemy dropped; many others screamed out as lead balls slammed into their bodies.

The British officer leading the attack ran among his decimated troops yelling, "Retreat! Retreat!"

Nate expertly reloaded his musket and took careful aim. The muzzle of the musket slowly followed something. BANG! The officer shouted with pain and grabbed his bleeding leg but continued to lead the retreat.

"Gracious Lord! That's the best shot I ever seen!" shouted the pudgy man.

"Luck," Nate shrugged.

It was not luck. Nate knew he could have put a musket ball in the officer's head, but something made him lower his aim. Fighting for his life was one thing; shooting a man in the back, enemy or not, was quite another.

*****

Cornwallis spent most of the night and early morning alone, but, by ten, headquarters was a nonstop flurry of activity. A staff meeting resulted in high-ranking officers streaming from the cave with set jaws and an air of purpose. Other, smaller meetings were in constant progress. It was, James thought, like some important decision had been made, and now the officers were executing it. Unfortunately, James had not been summoned into Cornwallis's office even once, so he was in the dark about what was going on. He had taken in tea at midmorning but had been harshly dismissed by the overworked Cornwallis. James tried to overhear some of the exiting officers' conversation, but they were all in a hurry and left quickly.

By two in the afternoon, James decided that he would have to leave and scout around outside for information. It would not be as easy as before. The grotto was tightly guarded, but, as "His Lordship's man," James was confident he could invent some excuse. Then, General O'Hara, who had been out for hours, swept by James, parted the curtain, and went in to see the commander.

Aware that O'Hara would be a good source of information, James made the dangerous decision to eavesdrop on the two officers. As charged as the atmosphere was in the cave, he knew he would probably be shot on the spot if caught listening or even suspected of doing so. Yet, James could feel that whatever was going on was all-important, and getting to the bottom of it was something he had to do.

There were four soldiers in the outer area of the cave. Two were humped over ammunition box desks feverishly writing orders with quill pens. The other two were loading documents and papers into three large chests. The space was small, and all it would take was for one of the men to glance up and catch James standing too close to the curtain. All of the morning meetings had been brief, and James knew that, if he was to overhear something important, he had to act quickly.

James simply picked up a teapot and, with his back to the soldiers, poured it on the bottom of the curtain. He then kneeled down with a rag and tried to blot it dry. The busy clerks were not interested. Again, using his back as a shield, James carefully pulled back the edge of the thick curtain as he blotted it. He had missed the beginning of the conversation between Cornwallis and O'Hara, but he heard enough.

"How many sick and wounded?" Cornwallis asked.

"Over two thousand, sir," O'Hara responded.

"Leave them," Cornwallis said without emotion. "Extra horses?"

"Four hundred," O'Hara said.

"Kill them," said Cornwallis. "Anything else?"

"The servants and slaves who came over to us," O'Hara said. "Their number is well over a thousand."

"Leave them," Cornwallis said with less feeling than he had expressed for the horses.

James clenched his jaw at that, and then the general realization hit him. My Lord, he thought, the mighty British army is going to make a run for it!

"See here!" one of the soldiers said from across the room. "What are you doing there?"

"Lord, sir!" sputtered James. "Ole clumsy James spilled tea all over creation, but don't you concern yourself. I 'bout got it all cleaned up now."

The soldier shook his head and went back to work just as James stood and O'Hara exited through the curtain.

"Good afternoon, general, sir," James greeted the steely eyed officer.

"Not likely," O'Hara responded and walked at a fast clip from the cave.

James directed his mind back to what he had overheard. He had no details, but, if the redcoats were planning an escape, Lafayette needed to know. The problem was not getting out of headquarters; it was gathering information and getting it to the American lines alive.

There was no predicting where the next blast would hit so anywhere outside was as potentially deadly as anywhere else.

"His Lordship want some proper bacon," James said casually as he breezed past the guard outside the cave.

"What?" the guard said. "Stop there immediately!"

"If you want to go in there and tell His Lordship he can't have no good bacon, well, sir, you go right on in. Now, he a'n't in the best frame of mind I ever seen, but . . ."

The guard went a little wide-eyed and said, "No, no . . . pass."

"Thank you, sir," James bowed and stepped out into the street.

The town itself was a desolate landscape of gaping holes made by cannonballs. Most of the houses were destroyed or severely damaged. Livestock, wagons, roads, and fences were blown to bits. Bodies lay mutilated from the bombardment. And still the cannons roared and the ground shook with explosion after explosion.

James needed more information, but the soldiers on the streets and docks were harried, busy, and diving for cover every few seconds as the cannonballs crashed down. A few citizens were helping soldiers position an assorted jumble of boats in a line along the docks. James thought that, if he could make it down to that area, he might be able to glean information from a black man who was securing a sloop to a cleat. He stuck close to the buildings and moved along cautiously. BAM! BOOM! BAM! The American and French rounds crashed down relentlessly.

As he ran across an open area and reached the head of the docks, he heard mortars whistling his way and dropped flat to the wooden planks. WHOOSH! One of the shells slammed into the water with such force that a geyser thirty feet high spewed up into the sky. The cannon fire would not reach much past the immediate Yorktown harbor area, but the weapons had done damage over the course of the siege as the burned-to-the-water hulls of thirty-one British transports could attest.

Running in a crouch, James threaded his way between the soldiers, sailors, and civilian boat workers who continued their tasks despite the exploding mortars. The black man, Frank, had secured the sloop and was now manually pulling a small fishing boat along toward its spot in the line. Without being asked, James grabbed onto the line and helped glide the craft toward a support pole where it could be tied.

"Why all these here boats a'bein' lined up?" James shouted over the artillery noise to Frank.

"Somebody 'bout to cross on over that water, but I'm guessin' it won't be none'a us."

A house near the water exploded, and they heard screams.

"The army is going to Gloucester?" James shouted over the increasing din.

"There a'n't nobody much else left in Yorktown," Frank yelled. "Less you count us Negroes, and I doubt'n they countin' us. I reckon the redcoats'll fight their way through that piddlin' group'a patriots over there and then move on up to New York."

"There a'n't enough boats to move'm all over there," James said into Frank's ear.

"Oh, they got more a'comin'," Frank replied loudly through cupped hands and pointed to the river.

James looked out and saw eight more boats of varying size and design sailing toward the docks.

"They won't do it in one trip, but they'll move a lot of'm fo it over wit. Maybe they take me along since I know my way 'round a boat."

"Luck to you, brother," James shouted and ran back down the dock toward the street. He successfully made it across the open space to the row of crumbling houses and businesses.

As he passed a brick storage building, he heard a shout.

"James! James! Come in here!"

The voice was familiar . . . Miriam!

Three-fourths of the roof and an entire side of the building had been demolished by an earlier blast. James stepped over a pile of rubble and picked his way across the floor that was strewn with shattered kegs of nails, broken boxes of fabric, and shards of glass. Miriam and ten other black people were huddled in the furthest corner that still had its sides intact and was covered by a portion of the roof.

"What in the world you doin' down here?" a shocked James asked Miriam. "In the middle'a all this?"

"Stayin' out the way all them cannonballs, which is more'n I can say for you out there runnin' 'round in all dat like a crazy man."

Despite the dire circumstances, both of them smiled. They each somehow felt reassurance at seeing the other. BOOM! The others scrambled deep into the corner, but Miriam and James continued to stand face-to-face.

"This will get worse," James said and looked right into her eyes. "You oughta git away."

"Our boat be leavin' here soon," Miriam said with conviction.

"Who told you that?" James asked.

"Captain Tompkins," Miriam replied defensively. "I seen him a day or so ago, and that what he say. Why, the man promised me right there fo God."

James continued looking into Miriam's hopeful face and could not bring himself to tell her she would not be going on the boats.

"I'll be a cookin' fo them British boys all the way up to New York City. Why, I might even sail on over to London, England, and bake up some mutton for His Majesty hisself," Miriam said.

"That sounds mighty fine, I must say. I was jest wonderin' though . . . you got somewhere else to go if that don't work out for one reason or t'other?"

"If I don't go with the redcoats, sooner or later I be sent up to Philadelphia all chained up and give back to that devil woman and spend rest'a my days bein' beat wit a ax handle. That where else I got to go."

At that moment, a cannonball struck a rock embedded in the slope leading down toward the houses. The solid cast-iron projectile bounced and came down on a stretch of cobblestone thirty feet from where James, Miriam, and the others had taken refuge.

James reached out and took Miriam's huge hand and looked straight into her eyes.

He said, "Miriam, you should know . . ."

BLAM! CRASH! The cannonball bounced off the cobblestone and smashed through the brick wall less than six feet from where Miriam and James were standing and continued on, ricocheting around the space.

Nails, glass shards, and bricks flew around like bullets in a tornado. The high wall collapsed inward creating a big, dense cloud of brick dust. The twelve-pound ball finally rolled to a stop against the far wall. Then everything went dead still.

*****

As the sun was going down, a rider was dispatched to the field from General Lafayette's tent.

"Nate Chandler!" the rider shouted as he rode up to where Nate and the others were, at last, having a rest and a meal.

"Here," Nate said and stood.

"You're to come with me," the rider said and extended his hand to help Nate up behind him on the horse.

"Why?" Nate asked.

"Orders from General Lafayette."

The boy swung up behind the rider, and they galloped away from Nate's impressed mates. Rex broke into a run and kept pace with the horse.

"I have one more mission of a secret nature that I am in great hopes you will undertake." Lafayette sounded almost apologetic. "You are not, however, obliged."

"I will make attempt to do whatever you wish me to do, sir."

"To no surprise," the French general said with gratitude. "Now, word has come to us from the other side of the river that boats are gathering at Yorktown. I want you to, as the farm boy, make your way down there and see what is transpiring."

"Of course, general."

"And, more importantly, come back with the information."

"Yes, sir."

"You will be walking directly into the line of fire of a hundred cannons."

Nate swallowed hard and said, "I am quite fast on my feet, sir."

"Bon courage!"

As darkness fell, Nate pulled himself up from a patriot trench, and he and Rex began running toward a town illuminated by a flaming orange and red hailstorm of death. They reached the road leading down to the waterfront and stopped in the shadows so Nate could figure out how best to proceed. Despite the danger they were exposed to, Nate was reassured by his dog's presence.

He rubbed Rex's head and said, "I guess it's just you and me again."

They pulled back further off the road and crouched behind a big supply wagon that had been flipped onto its side by an earlier cannon blast. They watched silently as three hundred British infantrymen marched down the hill and toward the waiting boats.

BLAM! A shell exploded at the rear of the British column. Fifteen infantrymen went down.

"Keep moving!" shouted a sergeant. "Keep moving!"

The wounded were abandoned, and the troops continued the double-time march down the hill.

Nate and Rex eased out onto the road and through the dead and badly wounded men. A British soldier whose left leg was gone looked up at Nate with terrified, pleading eyes.

"Help me," he rasped.

Nate looked down at the soldier, who wasn't much older than himself. He did not look like an enemy in a red tunic. All Nate saw was a boy dying alone on a muddy, bloody road thousands of miles from home.

"I wish I could help you," Nate choked and took the soldier's outstretched hand. "Don't concern yourself. The good Lord will walk with you now."

The boy died, but his eyes remained open. Nate closed them, said a little prayer, took a deep breath, and pushed on. It was hard to do, but he took two pistols from another of the dead men and stuck the weapons in his belt.

There was so much activity that Nate did not even try to be stealthy. Ignoring the falling cannonballs and explosions, he and Rex completed the trip down the slope and out onto the waterfront. It was bedlam. Soldiers were being hastily loaded onto boats big and small that had just returned from ferrying their first load over to Gloucester Point. The regular infantry and a few dragoons were acting as hard-nosed traffic wranglers and kept the soldiers moving and everyone else away.

Rex led as they threaded their way along the street that was now more an obstacle course of gaping holes, piles of debris, and bodies. But the destruction was not what filled Nate with apprehension bordering on panic. The soldiers getting onto the boats did that. The British army was escaping! After all of the logistic brilliance of the American and French generals, the bravery of the soldiers, the ever-tightening noose around Cornwallis and his men, they could not just vanish across the water into the night! No!

Maybe . . . maybe . . . yes! If the French cannons at the northwest redoubts could be hastily moved to the point of land jutting out above the York River, they could pick off the boats like sitting ducks as they sailed across to Gloucester. He must climb the steep slope up to flat land, run the mile to the French positions, and sound the alarm. Just as he started sprinting toward a path up the hill . . . BOOM! . . . a mortar struck the ground nearby, and the percussion threw him down and against a wall. He was not injured, but where was Rex? The dog had been at his side when the round hit.

Nate looked up and down the street, but there was no Rex.

"Rex!" he shouted. "Rex!"

No sign of the dog.

"Rex! Where are you? Rex!"

The animal did not appear, but Nate thought he heard his bark. He had no time to waste! Where was that dog? A series of barks came from the ravaged building right in front of him. Nate carefully entered, and, in the light of multiple small fires, he saw several bodies and his dog digging feverishly at a big pile of bricks and rubble.

"What are you doing?!" Nate shouted as he ran over to the dog. "Let's go!"

But Rex would not obey and continued to dig away at the bricks. It was then that Nate saw a big black hand emerge from the pile and push away some bricks.

It took only a minute for Nate and Rex to clear away the mound of wood and bricks. James lay dazed under Miriam's massive arms. Her solid, powerful body had shielded him from the worst of the blast. They were both completely covered in fine red dust.

"James!" Nate exclaimed. "James, is that you?"

James spit out a mouthful of dust and mumbled, "It what left of pitiful ole James."

Nate kneeled down and moved Miriam's limp arms from James's head and then tugged his friend from the pile.

"Are you injured badly?" Nate asked, looking over his battered friend.

James wiggled his toes and moved his legs. His arms and hands seemed intact.

"Thank you, Lord," he said and looked up. "Yes, I think I'm jest fine thanks to . . . Miriam!"

He crawled over next to the big woman who had saved his life and held her big head in his hands.

"Oh, Lord, oh, Lord," he gasped. "You a'n't s'posed to go away from me, woman. Oh, Lord, rest her precious soul."

"A good woman?" Nate asked sympathetically.

"Yes," James replied softly and crossed Miriam's arms over her chest.

"I must go," Nate said. "The redcoats are trying to escape over the river."

James stood shakily and took a deep breath.

"Yes," he said.

"The French cannons can stop them, but I have to get them word," Nate said with conviction.

"I'll go wit you."

BOOM! BAM! CRASH!

Nate looked down at Miriam and then at James.

"You do not have to go," he said.

"Yes, I do," James said and took another deep breath.

He closed his eyes for a second and touched Miriam's cheek. Then the slave, the boy, and the dog left the building and walked into a mob scene.

At least four hundred former slaves were pushing and shoving their way through the destruction and exploding mortars toward the boats along the docks.

"You promised!" a big black man screamed at Captain Tompkins, who was in the thick of the action. "You promised!"

A large group of slaves then surged forward. Infantrymen and dragoons drove them back with their swords. Many of the desperate men, women, and children went down for good under the swinging blades.

"Captain!" James shouted above the noise.

"Why aren't you with His Lordship?!" Tompkins shouted back.

"You told them that, if they come to your side, they'd be free!"

"They are!"

"Not if you leave'm here! They'll be sent back wit their masters. Slaves again, only beat and whipped slaves!"

"There's no room for them!"

A huge black man charged at Captain Tompkins, and the young officer shot him in the chest. The black man fell dead to the ground.

"Out of my way!" Tompkins yelled at James. "Or, so help me God, I'll kill you as well!"

James looked ready to attack the armed captain, but Nate grabbed his arm and pulled him away.

"You can't help them," he said to the slave.

James rubbed his neck and nodded, "I know, but . . ."

"Look!" the boy yelled. "The time is approaching!"

It looked like about another third of the British troops were on the boats.

"It will require one more trip after this one," Nate said in a frantic voice. "Lafayette can move the guns here and blast them from the water. Let's go!"

"Nate," James said calmly. "Nate."

"Yes?"

"We too late. It take most of a day to move them cannons over here. Them soldiers be all on the other side by then."

"No!"

"Yes. They'll get over."

There was no naval precision in the way the mismatched armada went into motion. With the wide disparity in size and sail, the vessels bumped into each other and got tangled in traffic at the docks. The soldiers, many inexperienced with boats, were not helping matters. Frank was the hardest-working man on the docks, darting from boat to boat trying to get them free of each other and their lines. At last, the final boat floated free of the dock. Frank took his chance and leaped onto its crowded deck. A British sergeant cracked his musket stock against the black man's skull, and he went over the side. He floundered for a few seconds and then emerged near a dock support. The look of rage and despair on his face was not cooled by the water.

With wildly divergent speeds and skill levels, the flotilla spread out and set full sails and oars for the short trip across the York River.

"I must do something!" Nate shouted over the din to James. "If only one cannon . . . something!"

James knew it was pointless, but the look on Nate's face told him the boy was going to go to the French batteries no matter what logic he used.

"We can try," he said.

The trio maneuvered through the waterside chaos and started climbing up the slope. Their route was steep and slick with matted foliage, twisted vines, and patches of loose dirt. Halfway to the top, a fine mist settled on them and almost instantly made the footing even more slippery.

Another few yards of climbing and the mist turned to big raindrops that came down in sheets. Nate and James were slipping and sliding and began to lose ground with each step. Rex managed to claw his way forward, but even he slipped partially back downhill when he lost traction on a stretch of shiny mud. The rain grew violent and was now being blown up from the river by powerful gusts. Crawling, grabbing onto roots and branches, Nate and James were trying to follow Rex toward the top when Nate fell into an artillery hole. James leaned down, extended his hand, and pulled the boy up and out.

The wind had started howling so loudly that they had to shout into each other's ears to be heard. The rain was now coming at them horizontally like little bullets.

"We must keep going!" Nate practically screamed over the wind to James.

"I can't see nothin' at all!" James hollered back.

"Just up! Up!" Nate yelled and took a long lurching stride but slipped, rolled over, and began sliding down a muddy track. James splayed out flat and caught Nate's shirt as he sledded by.

"We must wait this out a bit," James shouted.

The wind sounded like a wild animal.

"No!" Nate hollered and grabbed onto Rex. "I'm going on! They'll not escape!"

He wiped at the water and mud on his face and then looked through the rain back down toward the river. There he saw a sight to behold. His mouth dropped open, and he just stared in wonder. It took him a few seconds to process, comprehend, and believe.

"Look, James! There!" Nate shouted excitedly.

"Lord have mercy," James said with disbelief.

The Lord had mercy. The storm was even more powerful than they had realized. The freakish squall began shortly after the second group of British soldiers had left on the boats and was creating major havoc. The boats were being blown downriver, capsized, torn apart, and scattered. The thundering wind manhandled the smaller boats, ripping sails and tearing tillers from inexperienced hands. Many of them were practically thrown up onto shore near French positions, and the hapless occupants were promptly captured. The monster wind flipped other ships onto their sides or completely over as if they were sticks of wood. The larger boats that stayed upright lost all navigational control, and they were hopelessly scattered all over the river.

Incredulous, disbelieving, Nate and James watched the hopes of the British army go down in a swirling heaven-sent storm.

"Now, a'n't that sumpin' to behold?" James said, rubbing his head in wonder.

"The rat is in the trap," Nate grinned, his arm around Rex. "We must tell the general."

After savoring the storm and its incalculable gift for a few more minutes, they struggled up the slope and out onto open land. The French and American cannon fire continued unabated, so the trek was no safer than before. The mortars dropped on unoccupied fields and woods as often as they made a direct hit on a building or troop encampment. The unchecked fires burning everywhere cast an eerie glow over the landscape.

James, Nate, and Rex stopped behind a mound formed by some previous digging and looked out at the wide expanse of open space between themselves and the patriot lines. The forward-most British trench bisected the area like a battle scar. There was a lot of activity around the area.

"I wonder why them boys a'n't down there waitin' for a boat ride?" James whispered. "A'n't like they'd know there a'n't no boats no more."

"Look. I think they move that very way now."

Close to a hundred British soldiers came up out of the trenches and went into a loose formation. A small-framed sergeant in what could have been a green tunic shouted in the dark:

"Run ye bleaty little lambs unless you desire to miss the boats and be roasted on a skewer by the French or eaten raw by the bloody Americans!"

That was enough incentive for the soldiers. They just wanted to leave. Foregoing discipline and order, the hundred men broke into a full run across the open space. The sergeant ran alongside the stampede shouting insults and, less often, encouragement.

James and Nate knelt down behind the mound as the desperate British passed and continued on toward the hill that would take them down to the water and, they thought, their way out. Nate and James kept their heads down, but Rex suddenly went crazy. His bark was loud, constant, and frenzied, and he tugged against

Nate's hand on his collar with all of his considerable strength.

"Rex! Hush! Stop it!"

The barks turned into a bone-chilling howl so loud that it pierced the battle sounds.

Now twenty yards away, the sergeant stopped and looked back over his shoulder. His face was illuminated by a flaming split-rail fence.

There was a brief lull in the cannon fire.

"Slimy vermin!" Nate screamed like a demon. "Now you pay! You'll pay for everything!"

The passionate shrieks cut through the momentarily quiet field.

Clinton Adickes squinted at the boy standing on the dirt mound holding a pistol with both hands. Then he laughed.

"The crab crawled back from the briny deep he did!" Adickes shouted. "No matter! In a moment or two, your head will be bouncin' down the glen alongside the ugly carcass of your mangy animal."

He raised his sword and pulled his pistol from his belt.

"I await your charge!" Nate shouted.

"Wait no more!"

Adickes laughed like a madman while swinging around his sword and pistol and began advancing toward Nate. Nate coolly leveled the short English pistol and waited. Adickes stopped and leveled his own pistol.

BLAM! BLAM! Both of the notoriously inaccurate guns fired at the same instant. The lead ball from the dragoon's weapon came so close to Nate's head that it shredded the edge of his hat. The projectile from the boy's pistol was also wide.

At that precise moment, a wheel on an American cannon collapsed just as the weapon fired. The barrel tilted over, and the three-pound iron ball went only a few feet before it struck the hard ground and began skipping along across the field like a flat stone on a smooth lake. After its third low bounce, the cannonball crashed into Adickes's legs. He went down screaming and cursing!

The sergeant was writhing in pain but went still when Nate held the other pistol under his chin and Rex stood over his face snarling and drooling with rage.

"Your stay on this earth is over," Nate said.

Adickes's response was unexpected. Instead of spouting out a profane tirade, he started to cry and beg.

"Don't do it! I beseech you," he blubbered. "True, I be not much good and might well have done my share of misdeeds, but," he was really sniffling, crying tears, and looking pitiful now, "my mam counts on my little pay and lo what will become of her if her only son is shot like a rat?"

He called up all of his reserves and let out a pathetic wail.

"Oh, please don't kill me! Please! For my mother's sake! Please!"

Nate stared down at the monster feeling not a bit of sympathy.

"You won't get much out'a killin' that thing," James said disgustedly.

"He must die." Nate tightened up on the trigger.

"No, no, no, no," Adickes begged.

"Oh, you might get some little pleasure out'a it for a hour or so, but, after a while, it'd start a'botherin' yo head. Shootin' this man whilst he all tore up and don't have no weapons and all, it'd bother you 'til you meet your maker yourself."

"There is not much else to be done with such a sorry sort."

"He a'n't got no legs now. Let'm crawl on off and live like the snake he be."

Nate stared down at Adickes. The man's legs were crushed and twisted far beyond repair. If he lived, he would be a cripple for life. Nate aimed down the pistol, and the dragoon clasped his fists to his throat like a small girl and blubbered some more.

"I beg you, beg, beg, beg," he whined.

"Crawl away to your filthy hole and beg decent citizens for shillings," Nate hissed. "Go!"

Sergeant Adickes raised up on his elbows and began pulling himself along the ground. He left a snail-like trail of blood and fluids in his wake. Nate and James watched him slither off into the fire-illuminated night.

"I'm tired," Nate said.

"Me, too," James replied and draped his arm around the boy's shoulders. "I tired of the whole wretched thing."

The three of them walked slowly across the now-empty field toward the patriot camp.

*****

No one was tired the next morning when a British drummer and officer appeared at the top of a breastwork. The drummer played parley, and the officer carried a flag of truce and Cornwallis's offer to surrender.

A few hours later, a cease-fire was called so that the opposing sides could work out the surrender terms. Yorktown went silent.

“Listen,” James said as he, Nate, and Rex sat by a tent eating chicken.

“For what?” Nate asked.

“The birds,” the slave responded. “They back and they singin’. Them birds . . . they know it over.”

Epilogue

"*Mon Dieu!* That will not do at all," Maurice, Lafayette's valet, said as he pinned a seam in Nate's tunic. "We cannot have you holding the bridle of General Washington's horse looking like a chimney sweep, *n'est-ce pas*? And stand up straight!"

Nate complied good-naturedly. He did not enjoy being fretted over, pinned, and tailored, but Maurice had a good point. The boy had been thrilled when a patriot major came to his tent with the news that, through General Lafayette's recommendation, Nate was to have the honor of steadying George Washington's horse during the surrender ceremonies. It would be a memorable moment, and he should look his best. If that meant enduring Maurice for a few hours, it was a small price to pay.

"Aha!" Maurice exclaimed. "Look there, my boy! That is a uniform that fits *cap-à-pied!*"

James had entered the tent, and he did indeed look resplendent. Already a victim of Maurice's endless fittings, the slave's uniform was immaculately tailored and blindingly clean. His brass-buckled shoes were polished to a high shine.

Nate executed a deep bow.

"A grand good morning, Your Lordship."

"So far, it's jest fine," James laughed.

He was as excited as his friend. He had been personally selected by Lafayette to hold the French general's horse during the ceremonies.

He had told Nate, "We be on the front row watchin' sumpin' nobody can't never forget. Nobody. Never."

"Where is Franklin?!" Maurice asked in a flustered tone as he finished up one last stitch on Nate's uniform. "We must make all three of you *de beaux hommes* in less than an hour!"

"Three?" Nate asked, and then his mouth dropped open.

A young servant, Franklin, walked in leading Rex. At least, Nate thought it was Rex. This dog's gold coat was shimmeringly clean, and he wore a fancy new collar adorned with one of General Lafayette's sword tassels. He looked quite regal.

Before a shocked Nate or James could comment, Maurice trilled, "*Dépêchez-vous!* I've done all I can do!"

James, Nate, and Rex turned to leave.

"And all of you! Stand up straight!"

As they held the horses' bridles and waited for the ceremony to commence, they did stand up straight, but Nate's and James's stomachs were in knots. As frightened and exhilarated as they had both been during battle and bombings, they felt even more excitement as they looked out over the surrender scene. For a mile, French troops lined one side of the road and American soldiers the other. The French wore dress whites made up of bright regimental facings, shiny black gaiters, and plumes; they flew silk battle flags. Matching the French in pride if not style, the American soldiers paraded in the only clothes they possessed. At one end of the lines, the American and French generals sat on their beautiful horses. Washington and Lafayette looked like gods, and the others were only slightly less impressive.

Nate's hands had not shaken before the charge on the redoubt, but they shook as he took the bridle of General

Washington's horse. James's breathing had remained slow and steady throughout the most stressful of spy and war situations, but it came short and shallow when he stepped up to hold Lafayette's black mount. There was something monumental happening, and every single person in the scene felt it. Even Rex sat stone still in front of Nate and seemed transfixed by the event.

Among the hundreds of civilian spectators gathered to witness the ceremony were Nate's parents and Miss Albright, who held the reins to her simple open carriage. Leaning heavily on a walking stick, William stood by the horse. Rachel reclined in the rear seat of the carriage. Both were smiling broadly.

French Admiral de Barras unintentionally broke the tension of the solemn proceedings. Barras, who was perfectly comfortable standing on deck of a ship in a hurricane, was very uneasy on the back of a horse. When his mount stretched to relieve itself, the admiral shouted, "Help! My horse is sinking!" The laughter of nearby officers was quickly suppressed.

At two o'clock in the afternoon of October 19, 1781, the British troops began marching out and between the French and American lines. Nate thought his heart would beat out of his chest. The pageantry and significance of it all was almost too much to take in. The British had their banners cased, and their band played a song titled "The World Turned Upside Down." Then five thousand British soldiers threw their muskets into a huge pile. Over two thousand other British troops were dead, wounded, or sick. Lord Cornwallis found it difficult to believe he had been defeated by American ruffians and "that French boy" and did not appear.

Cornwallis sent word that he was ill and dispatched General O'Hara as his deputy to surrender the sword. That resulted in a little game of chess. Ignoring the American party, O'Hara approached General Rochambeau to surrender Cornwallis's sword. The French commander stonily pointed across the road to the American commander in chief, Washington. O'Hara muttered an apology and offered the sword to Washington. The American general waved him aside to his deputy, General Lincoln. The latter reached out, touched the hilt, and told O'Hara to keep the sword. It was over.

The top British officers were spared the humiliation of arrest, and most, including Cornwallis, sailed for New York in a few days. Thousands of regular soldiers were marched off to incarceration.

Lord Cornwallis came to grips with his defeat and, a few days before he left Virginia, followed his gentlemanly inclinations and paid a visit to General Lafayette to express his respects. As he walked from his horse toward Lafayette's tent, he saw a boy in uniform and a big gold dog. Both looked familiar, but he could not be sure. Perhaps, he thought, he just looks like the farm boy who once roamed the British camp selling corn and singing.

A cordial atmosphere pervaded the French general's tent. Lord Cornwallis was generous in his praise and Lafayette humble in his acceptance of the kind words. After the initial pleasantries, the two powerful men sat down to a lavish meal.

Part of what had made Cornwallis such a successful commander over the years was his ability to disguise emotion and surprise. He did a commendable job of it when James, dressed in his custom-tailored American uniform, entered the room and began to serve. Their eyes met, and, although His Lordship's pupils widened and there was a slight tic in his cheek, there was no other reaction. Throughout the rest of the long meal, James was as unobtrusive and invisible as he had been in the English nobleman's service.

"More wine, Your Lordship?" Lafayette asked.

"I thank you, general."

James poured.

"Perhaps a few more oysters would be to His Lordship's liking."

"Indeed. They are excellent."

"Bon appétit."

James served.

It went on and on without a single reference to their past situation although both were acutely aware of it. Lafayette seemed to enjoy the dance but made no comments on the subject.

As the meal ended and the two generals were saying their farewells, Cornwallis hesitated a second and cut his eyes over to James. Although people later said the slave must have been imagining it, James knew for certain that His Lordship, General Charles Cornwallis, had given him a trace of a smile and a salutatory wink.

After Yorktown, the British lost their will to fight, and it was essentially all over. Another two years passed before the Treaty of Paris was signed in Paris on September 3, 1783, and the war officially ended. American independence, declared on July 4, 1776, was finally secured.

*****

"Cows, Rex! Cows!" Nate shouted from Milk's back and held up his herding stick.

Completely happy, Rex whipped around the small herd and kept them moving. At the personal urging of General Lafayette, the Virginia General Assembly had awarded Nate five hundred dollars. He used a portion of the money to purchase eleven Devon cows. To the boy's astonishment, he had also been deeded the two hundred acres adjacent to his burned-out family farm, land he had not seen in almost a year, and a horse of his choosing, which was, of course, Milk.

The big draft horse was harnessed to a wagon full of basic tools and supplies. Although she looked very thin and frail, Rachel sat upright on the seat next to her husband, who had also lost a great deal of weight. His right leg stuck straight out and rested on the front rim of the wagon, and his walking stick lay against his thigh.

"We are getting very close, my dear wife," William said and turned in the seat to face her. "I hope the state of our home will not sadden you overly."

"We started from nothing once," Rachel said in a strong voice, "and we shall do so again."

"Indeed we shall," William said and patted her hand.

Nate held up the stick and pointed it to the right.

"Take them home, Rex! Take them home!"

The dog was very excited. He recognized the lane leading to the farm and could not get the cows turned and moving toward home fast enough.

"Peculiar thing," James mused as he walked alongside Milk. "Sometime it seem like we left here 'bout ten minutes ago and, then again, sometime it seem like twenty years."

"Much has happened since we last walked this road."

"The world's changed . . . a'plenty."

"You had a big hand in that, my friend."

"Aw, I didn't do much."

General Lafayette disagreed. The French hero wrote a certificate to the Virginia General Assembly that stated in part, "This is to Certify that the Bearer By the Name of James Has done Essential Services to me While I Had the Honour to Command in this State. His Intelligences from the Enemy's Camp were Industriously Collected and More faithfully deliver'd. He properly Acquitted Himself with Some important Commissions I Gave Him and Appears to me Entitled to Every Reward his Situation Can Admit of." Along with the certificate, Lafayette requested that James be given his freedom as reward for repeatedly risking his life in the patriot cause.

It took William, Nate, and James a month to get the fences repaired and a small log house constructed, which Rachel turned into a home in record time. Rather than wear them down, the constant hard work invigorated William and Rachel, and their health improved daily. William adjusted to his severe limp and forbade anyone from ever mentioning it again.

On a perfect spring afternoon, Nate and James sat up on the wildflower-covered hill and looked down at the small dwelling, peacefully grazing cows, and Milk. Rex sat with them, but his eyes never left the herd.

"This will be the finest cattle farm in America," Nate said.

"I got no doubts 'bout that," James responded and then went quiet for a while before he said, "'Bout time for me to move on."

Nate delayed responding for a few long moments before asking, "Must you leave?"

"Well, the war 'bout done and that's what Mr. Armistead give me the time to do. I oughta go back and see what else is in store for ole James. Might even be a free man one'a these days."

Nate looked at his friend.

"You aren't free yet, and the road is no safe place for a slave whether he is a hero or not. Keep your pass safe, stay out of sight, and get back to Mr. Armistead's quickly, you hear?" Nate paused. "I'll miss you, James."

"Aw, you might miss me 'round here gettin' in the way a little, but I a'n't really goin' nowhere."

He patted his chest right over his heart.

"You'll be wit me right in here."

"The same," Nate said.

They both reached out and rubbed on Rex.

After a few minutes, Nate said, "It was quite an adventure, wasn't it?"

"Yep."

They settled back and took in the Chandlers' three hundred acres of America.

Author's Note

Although this is a work of fiction, the stage on which the novel plays out is an accurate representation of the time. The battle scenes, topography and geography of the area, and lifestyles of the characters are based on historical documentation as are the movements and actions of historical figures.

James Armistead Lafayette was a real slave who acted as a double agent for General Lafayette. Except that he actually was on General Cornwallis's wait staff, the extent and detail of those activities are not specifically known, but the actions he performs in the novel are within the realm of possibility. General Lafayette did honor James, and the Virginia legislature did grant him his freedom as a reward for his services to the American cause, though not until 1786.

Nate Chandler and his parents are fictional but represent a fair picture of middling Virginia farmers during the eighteenth century. Nate's spy and battle activities are consistent with actions taken by spies and soldiers in the Revolutionary War.

The soldiers, servants, slaves, traders, rich and poor, and other background players that populate the tale are also characters one easily could have come across in eighteenth-century Virginia. Although individually fictionalized, their clothing, actions, style, and speech patterns are based on historical writings.

The timeline of the events described is mildly compressed in some instances as a nod to compelling action. But, the defining moments of the time and the book—the battle of Green Spring, Washington's march from New York, Lafayette's contributions, Cornwallis's movements, the occupation of Yorktown by the British and allied American and French forces, the battles and surrender—are accurate. Perhaps the most amazing event, the sudden and violent squall on the York River that sealed off the British escape and led to their surrender to George Washington, is true.

Even though Rex is fictionalized, I can only hope there was a dog like him around when the boys needed him.

Revolutionary War Time Line

1770	
March 5	Boston Massacre—British guards fire into a Boston mob, killing five and wounding six.
1773	
December 16	Boston Tea Party—In response to the Tea Act, patriots disguised as Indians dump three hundred chests of tea into Boston Harbor.
1774	
September 5	The first Continental Congress meets in Philadelphia.
1775	
April 19	The Revolutionary War begins when British troops exchange gunfire with Massachusetts minutemen at Lexington and Concord.
May 10	The second Continental Congress meets in Philadelphia.
1776	
July 4	The second Continental Congress adopts the Declaration of Independence.
1777	
July 31	The marquis de Lafayette receives rank from Congress as a major general in the Continental army.

1778

February 6	A treaty of alliance is signed with France.

1780

July 10	General Rochambeau, with 5,500 French soldiers, arrives in Rhode Island and joins General Washington's Continental army.

1781

May 10	British general Cornwallis and his troops arrive in Virginia.
July 6	The battle of Green Spring is fought near Jamestown, Virginia.
August 2	Cornwallis's army occupies Yorktown, Virginia.
September 5	The battle of the Capes is fought between the French and British navies. The battle is not decisive, but the battered British navy departs for New York, leaving Cornwallis without naval support and the French navy in control of the Chesapeake Bay.
September 14	Washington and Rochambeau arrive in Williamsburg and join General Lafayette.
September 28	The allied army marches from Williamsburg to Yorktown.
October 9	The allied forces begin bombarding the British forces at Yorktown.

October 16	Around midnight, Cornwallis tries to evacuate his troops across the York River, hoping to escape north. A dangerous storm foils the escape, and Cornwallis has little choice but to surrender.
October 17	Cornwallis signals for a cease-fire.
October 19	Cornwallis formally surrenders in what turns out to be the last major battle of the American Revolution.
1783	
September 3	The American Revolutionary War officially ends with the signing of the Treaty of Paris.

Historical Figures in the Novel

(Descriptions refer to the figures' status in 1781 during the American Revolutionary War.)

Civilians

James Armistead Lafayette (1760?–1832?)—slave belonging to William Armistead of New Kent County, Virginia. With Armistead's permission, James enlisted with the Continental forces under General Lafayette, who used James as a spy. In 1786, the Virginia General Assembly freed James as a reward for his service during the war. He changed his name to "Lafayette" in honor of the marquis de Lafayette.

William Armistead (1754–1793)—Virginia gentry planter who owned James. The Armisteads were a large important colonial family.

Thomas Jefferson (1743–1826)—governor of Virginia.

Continental and Allied Forces

General George Washington (1732–1799)—commander in chief of the Continental army.

General Rochambeau (1725–1807)—commander of the French forces in America.

Admiral de Grasse (1722–1788)—commander of the French naval fleet in America.

General Lafayette (1757–1834)—French general in the Continental army who, out of his desire to help American patriots, joined the fight even before France entered the war.

General Benjamin Lincoln (1733–1810)—George Washington's second-in-command at Yorktown.

General "Mad Anthony" Wayne (1745–1796)—general in the Continental army.

Lieutenant Colonel Alexander Hamilton (1755–1804)—secretary and aide to George Washington.

Admiral de Barras (?–c. 1800)—French naval officer.

British Forces

King George III (1738–1820)—king of England.

General Henry Clinton (1738–1795)—commander of the British forces in America.

Admiral Thomas Graves (1725?–1802)—commander of the British naval fleet in America.

General Charles Cornwallis (1738–1805)—commander of the British forces in the south.

General Charles O'Hara (1740–1802)—Lord Cornwallis's second-in-command at Yorktown.

Lieutenant Colonel Banastre Tarleton (1754–1833)—British dragoon.

Admiral George Brydges Rodney (1718–1792)—British naval officer.

Admiral Samuel Hood (1724–1816)—British naval officer.

French Glossary of Words and Phrases Used in the Novel

son appétit—his appetite

un assaut de surprise—a surprise attack

au contraire—to the contrary

Au revoir!—Good-bye! See you soon! Literally: until the next sight

avais-tu-peur—were you afraid

de beaux hommes—handsome men

Bien.—I understand.

Bon!—Good!

Bon appétit!—Enjoy your meal! Literally: good appetite

Bon courage!—Be strong! Literally: good courage

Bonjour!—Hello! Literally: good day

de bons agents secrets—good secret agents

cap-à-pied—from head to foot

célébration—celebration

la crête—the narrow ridge

Dépêchez-vous!—Hurry up!

une dette d'honneur—a debt of honor

en masse—as a group

entre nous—confidentially; between us

l'esprit de noblesse—honorable behavior expected of high rank

Excellent!—That's great!

faux—false

une force majeure—a major military force

une gêne de richesses—good fortune. Literally: an embarrassment of riches

guerrier—warrior

immédiatement—immediately

ingénieux—clever

je serai fier—be proud

merci—thank you

Merci beaucoup!—Thank you very much!

Une minute.—Just a minute.

Mon Dieu!—My goodness! Literally: my God

navire—ship

N'est-ce pas?—Right? Isn't that so?

Oui.—Yes.

en péril—in danger

la plus haute importance—of great importance

précisément—precisely

un prisonnier de guerre—a prisoner of war

le quartier général—military headquarters

Qu'est-ce que c'est?—What is this?

rapidement—rapidly

rétracter—to withdraw

une telle mémoire—quite a memory

validité—validity

About the Author

John P. Hunter is the author of *Link to the Past, Bridge to the Future* (2005), *The Last Neighborhood* (2003), *Birthmark* (1999), the Nickelodeon miniseries *My Secret Summer* (1992), and the award-winning documentary *Uttermost* (1987). He lives in Yorktown, Virginia.